The List

The List

Mikaela Musser

ARCHWAY
PUBLISHING

Archway Publishing books may be ordered through booksellers or by contacting:

Archway Publishing
1663 Liberty Drive
Bloomington, IN 47403
www.archwaypublishing.com
1 (888) 242-5904

Because of the dynamic nature of the Internet, any web addresses or links contained in this book may have changed since publication and may no longer be valid. The views expressed in this work are solely those of the author and do not necessarily reflect the views of the publisher, and the publisher hereby disclaims any responsibility for them.

ISBN: 978-1-4808-2966-4 (sc)
ISBN: 978-1-4808-2974-9 (e)

Library of Congress Control Number: 2016905135

Print information available on the last page.

Archway Publishing rev. date: 3/24/2016

Chapter 1

*C*ome on. *You can do this,* Gryffin thought, trying to get his courage together. This had never been a big deal before, so why was it now? From age three, Gryffin was known as a child prodigy when it came to performing. Playing music, writing songs, and getting up on stage were all incredibly easy to him. All these things came naturally to him. When he was on stage or even just playing for fun with friends, he felt at home. Music was his ultimate love. That is, until he met Emery.

Gryffin's hands began to tremble as he pulled his guitar pick from his back pocket. The small showroom was full of people. Some were familiar faces who had been to Gryffin's shows multiple times. Others were complete strangers who probably came with their friends to listen to some young rock group play a set. He had been on the stage for only a few moments and was already sweating profusely. Why was he so nervous? The lead bassist, Alec, gave Gryffin a pat on the shoulder and mouthed, "Are you okay?" It took a moment for Gryffin to register what Alec had asked. When he understood, Gryffin nodded. He surveyed the crowd, a sea of so many faces, so many people who came to hear them play.

Normally, he couldn't care less if he disappointed them. All he wanted to do was play music. Tonight was different. Tonight he had to play perfectly. Emery was somewhere in the crowd, waiting for him to sing. He wanted to make this the best show he had ever played. *Just breathe.* Gryffin closed his eyes and inhaled a deep breath. He opened his eyes and turned to the drummer, Paige, who was waiting to click off behind him. Gryffin gave her a small nod, and Paige knew exactly what to do. She tapped the hi-hat cymbal four times, and the band came to life. They played an upbeat song everyone could clap along to. As Gryffin let out the first lyric into the microphone, all he thought about was Emery. To fully understand why Emery was so important to Gryffin, we need to go back a few months, to a time when Emery was not yet in Gryffin's life.

Music has the ability to speak when words cannot be spoken. Melodies are created for one purpose—to take us on a journey to anywhere but here. It distracts us from reality and can impact our lives. At least that's how Gryffin Brooks felt every time he played a song. Gryffin picked up his guitar and slung the strap over his shoulder. Having the instrument in his hands made him feel at ease. A sense of peace overcame him whenever he played that first note. Much like every musician, Gryffin was a starving artist, paying his way through life with any and every gig he could pick up. He also fit the stereotype: long, shaggy rocker hair; ripped jeans; and always wearing a T-shirt of some kind. Gryffin didn't care about fame and fortune like the other musicians, though. He cared about the message. Gryffin thought if he could just inspire one person with his music, it would be worth all the money in the world.

Gryffin could play guitar for hours in his room. He didn't care that the neighbors would complain or that his fingers would bleed after a long jam session. All he wanted was to get what he was feeling out through the strings and maybe even through some lyrics too. The tune he played was soft and slow. He only played these types of songs on his special acoustic guitar his dad bought him for his tenth birthday. This guitar was Gryffin's best friend. It had been there for him through his first show with his band to his mother and father's car accident two years ago. This guitar held many secrets within its strings.

Time seemed to mean less and less to Gryffin with each strum he played. The clock said two o'clock one moment, and the next it was midnight. Not long after, Gryffin looked back at the digital clock and realized it was three thirty in the morning. Then came the knocking at the front door.

"Oh great," Gryffin mumbled as he finished his last note. Gryffin undid his guitar strap and sat his oldest friend on the stand. The rapping at the door continued. Gryffin quickly unlocked the door and opened it, already knowing who he would see.

"Mr. Brooks," a middle-aged, balding man boomed from the other side of the unopened screen door.

"How are you, Mr. Raymond?" Gryffin asked.

"I wish I could say well, Mr. Brooks. I have a sleep-deprived wife who won't stop complaining about the noise coming from your apartment. Just like every other night of the week." Gryffin shook his head. "Can you please, for the love of humanity, keep it down? Some of us have jobs to get to in the morning!"

"I understand, sir. I'm sorry," Gryffin said. "I just get so lost in the music. One minute I'm writing the start of a new song, and the next—"

"The next you have an angry neighbor begging you to stop keeping up his cranky wife." Mr. Raymond waved him off.

"Can you blame me though, sir? I mean, music is incredible. It holds so much power and inspiration."

"Yeah, yeah." Mr. Raymond wasn't buying it.

"Haven't you ever been inspired by art? Wanted to dance and let loose to the beat of a song? Or sing along to a lyrical masterpiece that gets stuck in your head?"

Mr. Raymond paused before answering. "I'm going to let loose my German shepherd if you don't stop cutting it out before midnight."

Gryffin smiled nervously. "Right. I'll make sure I set an alarm or something."

"Uh-huh," Mr. Raymond grumbled as he walked back to his apartment.

"Have a good night, Mr. Raymond!" Gryffin shouted down the hallway after him. Mr. Raymond shot him a glare. Gryffin realized how loud he had just been. "Sorry," he whispered. With that, Mr. Raymond disappeared inside his apartment and locked the door behind him.

Gryffin plopped into bed after he showered and ate a bowl of cereal. Before he drifted off to sleep, he looked through the notebook lying on his bed. It was full of songs he'd written over the past two years or so. He always had a writing utensil handy on the nightstand next to him just in case a new idea came to him in the middle of the night. Gryffin fell asleep in the middle of reading his latest lyrics. The song was about making something out of nothing, a belief he felt strongly about. Most if not all of Gryffin's songs were in the realm of hope and persistence. Even though Gryffin would disagree, he had never written a bad song in his life.

At noon the next day, Gryffin rolled out of bed to start the day. As a part of his daily routine, Gryffin laced up his running shoes and pulled on his gym shorts and a cutoff. He told himself he would run five miles but halfway through decided he was hungry and gave up at three instead. For breakfast, he made toast, crispy bacon, scrambled eggs, and a tall glass of orange juice. He scarfed down his meal and jumped into the shower. After that, he put on a fresh pair of clothes—well, clothes that didn't smell dirty, to him at least—and played his guitar for a couple of hours.

Gryffin's band met in his friend's garage every other day. This friend also happened to be the drummer, Paige. That's where Gryffin headed next. He packed his electric guitar, acoustic guitar, and songbook into his car and headed to practice. On the drive, Gryffin listened to a little-known indie band that, in his opinion, only real musicians knew about. He blasted the music the whole ride to Paige's house. When he arrived, his band was already there, getting set up for another day of practicing.

"Brooks, you got an extra pick?" the other guitarist, Derek, asked as Gryffin walked into the garage. Derek was tall and lanky. He dressed the classiest in the band, refusing to wear a T-shirt to a show, choosing a shirt and tie instead.

Gryffin stopped and dug in his pants pocket to find another pick. He pulled out a light blue pick and handed it to Derek. "Try not to lose this one."

Paige's garage was a good size for a practice room. They had laid down mats and pieces of carpet so the sound would be soaked in and not echo as much through the concrete. There were amps everywhere. Some of them worked, but most of them were old and shot from when they first started playing. Two mic stands stood in the front. One was for Derek, and the other was for Gryffin. The two took turns singing lead. The drum set was placed in the back with a small, clear enclosure around it to improve the sound. This garage was where the band had started, and it would probably be the place where they finished.

"Did you finish that song you've been working on?" Alec asked. Alec was tall and broad. The rest of the band had to look up to make eye contact with him when they talked. He was sometimes known as the band's bouncer.

"Yeah, I think so." Gryffin took out his acoustic guitar and strapped it on.

"What do you mean, you think so?" Paige asked from behind her drum set. Paige was a short, petite girl no one would assume played the drums. The pink streak in her blond hair was the only telltale sign that she was into rock and roll.

"I mean I think it still needs some work, but I have the general chords and melody down," he replied as he tuned his guitar.

"Well, what about the lyrics?" Derek jumped into the conversation.

Gryffin gave them all a small guilty smile. "I kind of haven't finished them yet."

Paige rolled her eyes, "Of course, Mr. Perfectionist won't let us hear it until that's done either."

"I just want it to be ready for an audience, and I don't think it is yet. Why does it matter? I mean, it's an acoustic song, so it's not like you all have to learn it."

"We need one more song for the show at The Lift on Friday night," Derek said in his professional voice. He was the one who booked all of their shows. Basically, he was the manager.

"Well this song isn't ready. Can't I just play the acoustic song I usually finish the show with?" Gryffin didn't see the problem with that.

"If we have to. Our audience is made up of a lot of our regular fans. I don't want the show to be exactly the same every time," Derek said.

Gryffin scratched his head. "I'll keep working on the song so it's ready for the show we have in a month or so. Will that work?"

Derek and Alec exchanged looks, not pleased with this but remaining calm. "Yeah that's cool."

"Awesome. Now, can we please practice our set list?" Paige beat on some drums to signify that she was ready to play.

"On your count." Gryffin pointed to her.

"One, two, three, four." She hit the hi-hat cymbal with her drumstick.

The practice ran for a good six hours, including a pizza break and a random game of darts. When it was over, Gryffin repacked his car and headed back to his apartment. As he drove back, he was determined to finish the song he had been working on for a month now. The song was focused on love and how it feels to be in it. For some reason, he could not find a way to put it together. All night, Gryffin stayed up and worked on the lyrics, but nothing came to him. Not one line he thought up for the song stood out to him. He ended up falling asleep in his desk chair, with his songbook lying on his chest. Another hard day's work had passed for the musician.

Chapter 2

The next morning, Gryffin awoke to his cell phone buzzing by his ear. He was startled by the sound at first, his head snapping up and whipping around the room. When he realized it was only his phone, he lazily answered it without looking at the caller ID.

"Hello?" His voice was low and groggy.

"Gryff, I need you to come get me." The voice sounded distant and muffled, but Gryffin could make out that it belonged to a man.

"Marcus, is that you?" Gryffin stood up and stretched.

"I need you to get me."

"Okay, where are you?" Gryffin thought it odd that he avoided the question.

"I don't know, Gryff," Marcus said, his voice breaking.

Gryffin then knew what was going on. He took on a more serious tone. "Marcus, were you using last night?"

The line was silent for a moment. Marcus then said quietly, "Just a little …"

Gryffin ran his fingers through his hair. "I can't believe this! Marcus, you said you were clean!"

"I was, bro. I was. Just three weeks ago." He remained soft-spoken like a child who had been caught sneaking a cookie before dinner.

"You've been back on that stuff for three weeks?" Gryffin was appalled. It shouldn't have surprised him though. Marcus had done this so many times now. Still, Gryffin wanted to give his brother the benefit of the doubt every time he got clean.

"I'm sorry, bro. Please, can you come find me?" Marcus pleaded.

"Do you remember where you were last night?" Gryffin asked as he grabbed his coat.

"No."

Gryffin shook his head. "Okay, look around you. Are there any signs or landmarks that you can see?"

"Uh ... okay, there's a little corner place called Luke's Antique Shop."

"That's on the outskirts of town. I'll be there in twenty minutes." He knew exactly where it was. "Just don't move, okay?"

"Okay," Marcus agreed.

"I'll see you soon." Before Marcus could say anything else, Gryffin hung up the phone.

Gryffin had been Marcus's DD for about two years now. Ever since the death of their parents, Marcus had been lost in a haze of depression and confusion. He blamed himself for his parents' deaths. They had been driving down the highway when Marcus was arguing with them about going to a college visit. His father turned around to tell Marcus to stop yelling at his mother when he swerved into the other lane. They were hit head-on by an oncoming semi. Their mother and father died instantly, and Marcus barely survived. After that, he spiraled out of control. Using drugs, getting blackout drunk every night, and not being able to maintain a job was his normality now. And Gryffin was the one to pick him up when he was too out of it to remember his name.

The drive passed by quickly, mostly because Gryffin was infuriated with his brother's poor choices. He had taken him to several facilities, and nothing ever changed. There had been only one time when Gryffin thought Marcus was done using for good. He had been sober for four months and was finally in his right mind. But when the anniversary of his parents' deaths crept up, so did his need for an escape. Unfortunately, that escape started at a beer bottle and progressed to other more dangerous distractions. Gryffin was terrified that Marcus would shoot up with some drug and not wake up. All he wanted was his brother back—not this stoned, hopeless soul who couldn't afford a candy bar.

Gryffin saw a small shop on the left side of the road. Luke's Antique Shop was literally in the middle of nowhere. A man sat on one of the dividers in the parking lot. Gryffin pulled up to the spot next to him and parked the car. Marcus was a sorry sight. He was wearing dirty jeans, muddy shoes, and a tattered flannel. His hair was a tussled dark mess, and his face was unshaven. As Gryffin got out of his car and was able to get a better look at his brother, he noticed Marcus' bloodshot eyes. Whatever Marcus took last night still hadn't left his system.

"You came!" Marcus slurred in excitement.

"Of course," Gryffin replied. He put Marcus's arm around his head and slipped his other hand around Marcus's waist. "Come on, buddy. Let's get you home."

Marcus huffed as Gryffin pulled him to his feet. When he was standing, he took a small step back, his head spinning. "Whoa, man, I'm having a serious case of vertigo." Gryffin noted the burning scent of alcohol on his brother's breath.

"You're having a serious case of too much to drink." He continued to pull Marcus to the car. When they reached the passenger side, Gryffin opened the door and helped his brother into the seat. He strapped Marcus in and closed the car door behind him. After Gryffin had gotten into the driver's side, Marcus turned to him and said, "You're a real good big brother."

Gryffin just stared at him for a moment. Sadness for his brother overtook him. He tried to give a convincing smile and replied, "You too, buddy. You too."

The whole way back, Marcus babbled about everything under the sun. He laughed at things that didn't make sense and even cried once, talking about seeing a kitten in an alley. Gryffin was patient with him and let him talk all the way back to his apartment. Even though he hated that Marcus was destroying himself, he still loved his brother and would do anything for him. When they returned to Gryffin's apartment, Marcus crashed on the couch. Marcus didn't really have a home. He usually stayed at a stoner buddy's house, and Gryffin wouldn't hear from him for days, sometimes even weeks. Gryffin made enough off of shows that he could pay rent on his own. But he wouldn't mind the help from his brother. That was a long shot though, so Gryffin wasn't holding his breath.

Marcus slept the rest of the day and all night. Gryffin checked on him every few hours to make sure he was breathing all right. He didn't know for sure how much Marcus had to drink last night or what he used, so it was better to be safe than sorry. When Marcus checked out okay, Gryffin decided to keep writing his infamous unfinished song. He worked on it all day and late into the night. Again, nothing came to him. He finished out the evening rehearsing the set list he and his bandmates had put together for tomorrow night's show.

The sound of dishes clanking around in the kitchen awoke Gryffin. He squinted at the clock; it was 8:30 a.m. *So much for sleeping in today.* Gryffin slid out from under his warm, comfortable blankets. He swung his legs over his bed and headed to the kitchen to see what the commotion was. Marcus appeared to be making breakfast. Gryffin recognized the aroma of eggs on the skillet ... or was that *burnt* eggs on the skillet? Either way, it made his stomach rumble with a desire to be fed.

"Morning," Marcus greeted cheerily from the stove.

Gryffin rubbed the sleep from his eyes. "What are you doing?"

"I thought you might be hungry, so," he motioned to the pan full of dark scrambled eggs with a fork, "I made some breakfast."

Gryffin's apartment was extremely small. It was one bedroom, and the kitchen and family room were connected. The only bathroom was located right next to the front door in the kitchen. So it took four steps to go from his room to the kitchen/living room. This made the aroma of burning eggs extremely strong even in his room.

"Marcus, you don't need to do that." Gryffin pulled out a chair from the small wooden table a few feet from the stove and took a seat. Marcus went back to cooking. He was even making toast. Gryffin felt that this random act of kindness was under false pretenses. "Are you doing this because of what happened yesterday?"

Marcus stopped stirring the scrambled eggs in the pan. "Can't I make my brother some breakfast?"

Gryffin sensed a hint of defensiveness in his brother's tone, "No, no you can."

"Good." Marcus scooped some of the burnt scrambled eggs onto two plates and completed the presentation with a piece of toast to accompany the mess of protein. Marcus set the plates down at the table, one in front of Gryffin and one on the other side of the table. He then retrieved two forks from the drawer next to the refrigerator and set them beside the plates.

Gryffin eyed his food and then Marcus's face that was trying to express something of innocence. He decided it wouldn't be worth the fight. "Thank you," Gryffin settled on. Marcus smiled broadly, and the two boys ate, not saying anything as they engulfed their food. Being boys, they took about three heaping spoonfuls of eggs and two bites of their toast, and their breakfast was gone.

"So, I hear you have a show tonight," Marcus said after wiping his mouth with one of the many napkins lying in a pile on the table.

"Yeah, we're playing at The Lift at eight," Gryffin responded after swallowing a mouthful of crunchy toast. "Are you going to come?"

Marcus shifted uncomfortably, "Uh, no. I already have plans tonight."

Gryffin eyed Marcus suspiciously, "What kind of plans, Marcus?"

"Just some buddies and I are going to watch the game tonight."

"You hate baseball. You're hanging out with that Ray Mainely, aren't you?" Gryffin tried to hide the anger in his voice.

Marcus began getting defensive, sitting up on the edge of his chair as if to prove something. "So what if I am? He's my friend, Gryffin."

"No, he's your dealer. You buy crap off of him; I know it. I was there all the times you came off that crap and couldn't even remember your name. Just like yesterday morning!" Gryffin ran his fingers through his hair. He got up from the table and took a step away from the conflict at hand. After he took a moment to compose himself, he walked back to the table and rested his hands on the back of his chair. "Marcus, you know you're better than this. I know you've been having a rough time with, well, everything, but I've told you before, and I'll tell you again: I'm here for you, man. You're my baby brother. I'm going to do whatever I can to help you out."

Gryffin saw right through the macho act Marcus put on. He could see the desperation for something more than a quick fix under Marcus's rough exterior; his eyes screamed for help. For a moment, he thought he had broken through. He thought Marcus genuinely wanted to get better this time. But Marcus's face hardened as soon as these thoughts entered Gryffin's mind.

"I don't want your help. I can take care of myself, Gryff," Marcus snapped.

"Then please start doing it! You're going to kill yourself with this stuff!"

Marcus stood up and walked straight up to his brother, looking him dead in the eyes with a cold, lifeless stare. "Don't ever tell me how to live." With that, Marcus left.

Gryffin stood alone in his apartment. He had no idea where his brother was going to go next or what he was going to do. But one thing was for sure. Gryffin did not lose hope.

Chapter 3

*E*mery Everett was having just about the worst day possible. Her car had broken down before work this morning, which made her late to an important meeting with a client. That caused her client to pass up the house she had been showing them for weeks. To top that off, the drycleaner delivered her the wrong set of clothes at her office, making her late to yet another meeting because she had to sort that mess out. After the day she just had, Emery was ready to enjoy a meal at her favorite restaurant. Much to Emery's dismay, The Lift was bustling with customers. *Really?* She was ready for this day to just be over. All she wanted was a nice, quiet dinner at the grille down the street from her apartment. That obviously wasn't going to happen tonight.

Since the entire restaurant was filled, Emery was forced to sit at the bar. Emery hated sitting at the bar simply because she didn't drink and she didn't want to be around anyone who did. With a sour look, Emery eyed a vacant chair at the bar next to one other open seat. She took her seat, and when the bartender came over to her, she ordered her usual—grilled chicken salad with a glass of tea. The bartender nodded and smiled as he walked away to put in her order with the kitchen staff. Emery glanced around the large room to people watch. The Lift was dimly lit and decorated in an urban-rustic way. It was a laid back, comfortable place for customers to come in and have a good meal and enjoy the atmosphere. Emery liked the vintage vibe of the place.

To the back of the restaurant, there was a stage and a place for people to stand and watch the musical performance. Emery noticed a drum set, an acoustic guitar, at last three amps, and two microphones in stands on the small performance stage. *Oh great.* Emery knew then why the entire place was packed. It was a Friday night—the night The Lift had talent to entertain their clientele. *Why couldn't it just be a normal night?* Everyone would be cheering and singing along to whatever song this band would play. Emery could feel a migraine coming on just thinking about the chaos that was about to unfold when the show began. She rummaged through her purse to find some pain reliever. Her hands felt the pill bottle at the bottom of her bag. She pulled it out and popped a couple pills into her mouth. Hopefully this would take care of the premature headache.

A couple of minutes passed, and the bartender appeared with her sweet tea with a hint of lemon. He set it on a small logoed napkin in front of her and told her that her food would be out soon. She thanked him, and he moved on to his next customer. Emery hoped she would receive her meal before whatever band was playing went on. She was not in the mood for pep of any kind. Emery sat with her thoughts, feeling more serene than she had felt all day, even with all of the commotion surrounding her.

"Excuse me," a voice said from behind her.

Emery reluctantly turned around. A tall, well-built man around her age stood behind her. He flashed her a nice smile as she made eye contact with him. "Is that seat taken?" the young man asked as he pointed to the empty seat next to her.

"No, it's all yours," She motioned to the seat.

"Thank you." The young man took the seat next to her. From what she could see, he had a laid-back style. He had long, messy blond hair that swept across his forehead and was wearing holey jeans with a white T-shirt and dark gray Converse. There was something Emery liked about that look—it was edgy but with a dash of style. Emery realized she had been staring at him and started to read the labels of all of the types of alcohol on the shelves behind the bar.

"Can I get you something, sir?" the bartender asked when he saw he had a new customer.

"Just a water, please," the young man responded.

"No problem. I'll have that right up." The bartender disappeared behind the counter, and within a few moments, he was handing the young man a tall, cold glass of water.

"Thank you," he said and took a sip of his beverage.

Emery continued to read the names of the tall wine bottles in her head. The young man took a few more sips of his water.

"So, are you here to watch the band?" he finally said, breaking the silence between them.

"Oh, no, I didn't even know there was a band playing tonight. I just came to have a quiet dinner, but that isn't going to happen." There was a hint of aggravation in Emery's tone.

"You aren't looking forward to the first song then, huh?" the young man said.

"Not really, no. The bands they always have here are either extremely country, metal, or some type of emo punk. They all sound the same to me. Singing about lost love and everything someone else has already sung about before."

The young man chuckled. "Wow, you really don't like music, do you?"

"It's not that I don't like music; it's more of the fact that I've heard it all before."

"So, basically, it takes a lot to impress you," he inferred.

"I'm a tough one to crack." Emery nodded and took a sip of tea.

The young man seemed intrigued. "Are you always a ray of sunshine?"

Emery sensed his sarcasm and played along. "All day, seven days a week," She raised her glass to him.

"I think the band they have playing tonight might surprise you. I heard they're pretty good. Most of the people here tonight are big fans."

"Oh, you're a groupie, aren't you?" Emery laughed. "Well, sorry to disappoint, but I've heard it all."

"Why not just give them a chance?" the young man replied.

Emery paused a moment before answering. "Because whenever I give someone a shot, they let me down," she heard herself say. The young man did not speak. He just watched her. She realized she wasn't talking about the band anymore and brought her thoughts back to the conversation at hand. "I've just heard them all."

Before the young man could respond, a man on the stage made an announcement that the show was about to start.

"Well, I hope you stay and at least listen to one song. Who knows? You may actually like them," he said as he got up from his chair.

"Don't count on that," Emery joked.

The young man gave Emery a genuine smile. "It was really nice to meet you …"

"Emery Everett," she finished for him.

"Well, Miss Everett. Maybe I'll catch you after the show."

"Maybe," she replied.

The young man gave her a full grin and walked off into the crowd. It wasn't long after he disappeared that Emery realized he didn't give her his name. She took it as a sign that she probably shouldn't stay for the show. How was she supposed to find him after in this sea of people if she didn't even know his name? She scanned the crowd, looking for him. No luck. The bartender brought out her warm plate with a decent-sized piece of chicken and a bowl of salad. Emery wasn't naive enough to think that she would see the young man again, so she decided she would eat her meal and leave.

Just as she picked up her fork and knife, the crowd toward the back of the restaurant began to clap and whoop. *Here we go.* She watched the band come onto the stage and hook up their instruments. There were five of them. To her surprise, the drummer of the band was a girl. The others looked to be men in their twenties. The stage remained dark as the band members tuned their instruments. Finally the spotlights shone on the musicians. The bass player stood on the far left, a guitarist in the middle, and another guitarist on the right, with the drummer sitting directly behind them. From what Emery could tell, the guitarist on the right was the best dressed in the group. The bassist was big, and it looked like the veins in his arms would pop if he played his guitar too hard. The middle man was not facing the crowd yet. He was talking to the drummer. When he turned around, Emery got a good look at him.

"We are Escalates, and we want all of you to have a good time tonight!" the young man said. It was the same young man Emery had spoken to a short time ago. He looked back at the drummer, who beat four times on the cymbal, and the song began. Emery felt embarrassed that she had been talking to the band's lead singer about how much she was not looking forward to their performance. She wanted to take her food to go and sulk in her humiliation in the comfort of her home. But something made her stay. The song that Escalates was playing mesmerized her. She was enthralled by the lyrics and even found herself tapping along to the beat. Emery would never admit that though.

Escalante's sound was a branch off of alternative rock with a hint of indie and pop involved. Their songs were more fun and uplifting than the breakup songs Emery was used to hearing from other performers on that stage. The band played for a good hour or so, and Emery didn't want it to end. The young man she had met before had a wonderful voice. It was unique and captured the essence of every song he sang. Emery forgot she had food until the second to last song. When the Escalates announced that they were about to play their closing song, she scarfed down the last, now cold, pieces of her meal. The final song was different from the rest of the songs they had played throughout the night. This one was slow, and only the young man played it. He switched guitars for this song; instead of his red electric guitar, he picked up a mahogany acoustic guitar.

"This is a song I wrote a few years ago. It's called 'Still Here,'" the young man announced before playing. Emery loved the soft, intricate melody that the young man played. The lyrics were about losing someone and how things would still be different if they were still around. She wasn't sure what the song's meaning was, but she loved the message. The young man seemed to be entranced in the song he sang. He played with his whole heart, and raw emotion showed through his expression.

After the young man had finished the song, he welcomed his band back on stage, and they took a bow. The crowd went wild, and some of them even chanted the bandmates' names, asking for an encore. Emery found herself clapping along. She had to admit that he was right. She really did like Escalates. The band began packing up everything on the stage and taking it through the side door closest to them. Emery assumed they were putting their equipment in their van in the ally. When they came back in, they were bombarded with people who wanted to talk about their music or get an autograph. Escalates was apparently a big deal around town, and Emery had only just heard about them now. Emery did not see the young man come back in with the others from outside. She waited a few minutes to see if he would show. Then she overheard two guys asking the drummer where the lead singer was. The drummer said he was heading home because he had to meet up with his brother. Emery couldn't help but feel let down when she heard that the young man would not be making an appearance. Normally, she couldn't care less about other people. There was something about him though, something that made

Emery want to talk to him again. But it wasn't going to happen. Not tonight anyway. Disappointed, Emery decided to suck it up and pay her bill. Before she left The Lift, she took one last at the crowd of people just to make sure the young man hadn't changed his mind. Then she pushed through the front door and walked out into the parking lot.

Chapter 4

The parking lot surrounding The Lift was dimly lit with street-lights on each corner. Although it wasn't a large parking lot, if you forgot where you parked your vehicle, it would be hard to make out where it was. Emery always parked in the same spot, the far left corner where no one lingered. Everyone made a break for the front and middle spots. Emery liked to stay out of the way and avoid traffic on nights like this. A few cars pulled into spaces as she made her way to her small silver car. She could still hear the crowd talking and laughing inside the restaurant. As she was about to put her key into the door to unlock it, someone touched her shoulder. Emery gasped and turned quickly around, holding her key in a threatening position.

"Whoa, whoa! Sorry!" The young man put his hands up like he meant no harm. "I didn't mean to scare you."

Emery caught her breath. "Don't sneak up on me like that!" She held her chest with her free hand, steadying herself.

"I thought you heard me. I'm so sorry."

"It's okay. I was hoping a heart attack would creep up on me tonight," Emery said sarcastically. She put down her key from stabbing position and tried to relax a little. "What are you doing here? I thought you left."

"No, I was waiting for you." The young man smiled.

"Outside like a stalker?"

"I figured if you didn't leave during the show, you would leave right away after it was over. But I was wrong. I was about to go home when you finally came out."

"Well, sorry if I wanted to finish my meal." Emery had an excessive smarminess to her tone. "Thank you, by the way, for making me feel like a complete idiot."

"How did I make you feel like an idiot?"

"I went on about how much I thought the band wouldn't be good, and here I am talking to the lead singer." She crossed her arms. "You know, you could have told me you were in it, and I would have been saved from embarrassment."

"Okay, yeah, that was my bad. But you did stay for the performance." He hinted at a satisfied smile. "So, what did you think of us?"

"Oh no—no, I'm not about to give you an answer when you made me live through an hour of humiliation," she said, wagging her finger at him.

He tilted his head to the side and examined her for a moment. A huge grin crept onto his face. "You liked us, didn't you? You actually enjoyed yourself!"

Emery could feel heat rushing to her cheeks. "No, I never said that." He squinted at her as if he didn't believe what she said. Emery tilted her head back in exasperation. "Fine. Okay. You were good." She hated being wrong. "But don't let it get to your head, okay?"

"I'm totally doing that right now." He laughed.

"Great. Another egotistic musician. Just what the world needs." Emery shook her head.

"You are so warm and inviting. You know that?"

"I am just a realist, that's all."

"Why? What's so bad about trying new things and maybe even liking them?"

"Because when you try something, you have to take your walls down. I don't do that. People get hurt when they let their guard down," Emery answered. The young man stood, captivated by her. Emery grew uncomfortable. "What?"

"I have never met anyone quite like you, Miss Everett," he said, not taking his gaze from her. "I bet you can find something wrong with everything, can't you?"

"It's not that I'm negative or anything. I just see facts for facts and don't stray from them."

"So you don't use things, say, like your imagination?"

"I don't need to. What's the point? This is the world we live in. Why would we try to make it something it's not, forcing our hearts to yearn for the impossible?"

The young man's eyes narrowed. "What I'm hearing is that you don't have any fun."

"What? I have fun all the time." Emery tried to sound convincing.

"Fun like what?" the young man challenged her.

"Okay, like I go out to The Lift twice a week to get out of the house and talk to friends," Emery said, satisfied with her answer.

"The staff doesn't count."

Emery was caught. "What does it matter to you anyway?"

"Nothing, I just think it's sad that you don't enjoy yourself or the little things in life."

"Life isn't a friend. The sooner you stop acting like it is, the better off you'll be." The conversation simmered then, both of them not knowing what to say after that. Emery decided she was ready to get out of this awkward situation, "Well, I should probably go." She put her key in the lock and turned it.

As she did this, the young man eyed her curiously. He looked as if he wanted to say more but didn't know how. Emery closed her car door and started the engine. Just before she was about to put the gear in reverse, the young man knocked on her window. Emery lowered it slowly, and the young man leaned into the car a little so she could hear him.

"I think I could change that," he said.

"Change what?"

"Your view on life. I think I could make you see that not everything is all that bad."

Emery smirked. "And how do you plan on doing that?"

"I have some ideas. Meet me in the park tomorrow afternoon, and I'll show you."

"What if I don't?" Emery played along.

"Then the reoccurring thought of what might have happened if you had met me at the park will haunt you for the rest of your life," he said as he backed up from her car.

"Why do you care so much?" Emery didn't understand why he would go through all of this trouble just to get her to maybe have fun once.

He seemed to think for a moment before answering, "I think that everyone should see the brighter side. Nothing is really all that bad, you know." With that, he turned and began to walk away from Emery's car.

Emery watched him, trying to process what had just happened. *Did I just agree to meet this guy tomorrow afternoon? Am I okay with that?*

"Wait! What's your name?" Emery almost forgot to ask.

The young man looked back at Emery and with a smile said, "Gryffin Brooks."

For the first time in a long time, Emery smiled the whole way home.

Chapter 5

*G*ryffin could hardly sleep that night. Usually he was still going off of adrenaline from the show at this hour, but this time it was a different kind of restlessness. He was really looking forward to seeing Emery tomorrow. Gryffin thought about their meeting over and over again. The way her dark eyes were entrancing, how her long, dark hair fell perfectly over her shoulders and down her back. He liked her snarky attitude and the way she talked to him like she didn't care what he thought. Emery was tough, and Emery was genuine—qualities Gryffin didn't find in many people anymore.

Finally sleep overtook Gryffin's racing mind. He woke up early the next day to get his workout in and have enough time to get ready to meet with Emery. He wore a dark gray T-shirt, a nice pair of jeans, and his favorite pleather Converse. At a quarter to noon, he decided to head over to the park. Before he departed, he made sure to grab a crudely folded piece of paper that was shoved in the back of his desk drawer. This paper had seen a lot; it was wrinkled and frayed along the edges. Gryffin put it in his wallet. When he decided he had everything he needed, Gryffin left his apartment, locking the door behind him.

The January afternoon in South Carolina was warm with the sun beating high above, but it was complemented with a soft breeze that came from the east. Emery sat on a park bench toward the middle of a clearing. There was a jungle gym on a patch of cedar chips to the left of the entrance and a wooded area to the right. When you entered the park, you could park your car and follow the path around the landscape to run a mile or just walk. In the center of the park entrance was a large fountain, shooting strings of water into the air and back into the small pool of water surrounding it. Just beyond that was a clearing where you could have a picnic or sit and enjoy the scenery. A pond sat at the end of the park, far from the jungle gym so the children would have to run a good distance to get to it. Emery sat on one of the benches where she could get a good view of the shimmering pond.

What am I doing here? kept going through her head. She wondered why she was meeting a guy she barely knew just because he wanted to try to make her see things a little differently. *I must be crazy,* Emery thought as she waited for Gryffin. The sky was completely blue today, and big white clouds rolled passed above her. Even though the scenery before her was beautiful and full of chirping birds, she couldn't put her mind at ease.

"Miss Everett," Gryffin greeted cheerfully as he approached the bench.

Emery gave him a half smile, the best greeting she could give. "Gryffin Brooks." She nodded.

"I'm surprised you came." He scratched his head absentmindedly.

"Didn't think I would show?"

"I just thought you would chicken out," Gryffin retorted. "You know, because it's out of your comfort zone."

"Real nice." She rolled her eyes. Gryffin chuckled and took a seat next to her.

Emery decided to get to the reason why they were there. "So what's this master plan of yours that's going to make me this optimistic person?"

"Well," Gryffin began, "we have a quite a few things to do in order to give you that more cheery disposition." He pointed to her face. "Because this—this has got to go."

"This is my face," Emery said, appalled.

Gryffin smirked. "I mean you always look so serious and stone faced. You need to crack a smile—you know, be more approachable."

"Thanks for that."

"No problem." Gryffin smiled coyly.

"So you're going to get me from this," she motioned to herself and then to Gryffin, "to this."

Gryffin nodded proudly.

"Wonderful," Emery sarcastically said. "How?"

Gryffin shoved his hand in his pocket and pulled out his billfold. He flipped the dark leather wallet and pulled a warn piece of lined paper. He unfolded it slowly. "By this."

"What is that?" Emery eyed the paper curiously.

"It's a list of things we'll do." He brought the paper closer to him so Emery couldn't see. "And by the time we're done, you'll have an enlightened perspective on this wonderful thing we call life." He tucked the wallet back into his pocket.

Emery looked unimpressed. "Are you serious? A list?"

"Hey, I have to be organized. This is going to be a long process, Emery." Gryffin stood up. "Are you in?"

Emery examined him for a few moments, wondering if all of this was a waste of time. Then she realized she really didn't have much else going on other than her job. With a sigh, Emery stood up as well and said, "Why not?"

A big smile crept on Gryffin's face. "Really?"

Emery shrugged and nodded, flashing a somewhat convincing smile of her own. "What's first on the list, chief?"

Gryffin couldn't help but keep smiling. He glanced down at the list. "We need to borrow a boat."

The water rippled as Gryffin rowed the paddles through the large pond in the park. Unlike most city ponds, this body of water was clean and swimmable. The fresh smell of grass and air flowed through Emery's nostrils as they began their journey downstream. She wasn't sure how Gryffin had talked one of the fisherman at the park into using his boat, but he did. Maybe it was his charm; something about Gryffin made you want to do anything he said. He certainly had a way with words.

For the first few minutes, neither Gryffin nor Emery spoke.

They sat in silence, enjoying the serenity of the life around them and the melodic sound of the water swooshing under the oars as Gryffin pushed down on them. Around the pond were small patches of trees, shading the sun in some areas. This was perfect after they were under the sun for a few minutes, cooling them off to a more comfortable temperature. This was the most at peace Emery had felt in a long time.

After a few more strides, Emery decided to break the silence. "Why did you borrow a boat off of that older gentleman again?"

"To begin step one from the list." Gryffin continued to pull and push the oars on either side of the boat.

"And that is?"

"To enjoy nature for what it's truly worth," Gryffin answered.

"You want me to enjoy nature? Like camp or something?" Emery did not like the sound of that. She was not much of an outdoors girl. Usually, she limited her outside activities to trail runs and walking down the street from her apartment to The Lift.

"No, not exactly." Gryffin could see she was beginning to regret her decision. "I want you to spend some quality time outside with no distractions." The small, creaky boat slowed to a stop, just as Gryffin wanted it to. He pulled the oars inside the boat and set them down in front of him. Then he propped his elbows on his knees and leaned forward, examining Emery with curious eyes. "Hence why we need the boat. We are in the center of the pond; no one else is around us besides the fish and a couple of frogs. This is the most secluded part of the park, making it easier to focus."

"So … what am I supposed to do?" Emery didn't understand the point of this exercise.

"Take a deep breath," Gryffin instructed and took a breath. "Relax," he said. "Just take everything in. The beauty of the water, the swaying trees, the chirping birds. Let that control you for a while."

Emery cocked her eyebrow, unconvinced.

"I promise, you will have a different perspective on beauty and nature," Gryffin said.

"Okay, if you say so." She decided to give into his strange antics. After all, she had already come this far. Emery took a deep breath and closed her eyes for a moment as she released it. When she opened her eyes again, nothing had changed. The trees were still standing tall, the birds were still chirping, and the water was still rocking them a little. She expected something to reveal itself once she had done what Gryffin instructed, but nothing did. It was the same old pond in the same old park.

Gryffin was focused on the sound of the water underneath them. He loved the way it sloshed beneath the small boat and the way it felt to be floating. This was all amazing to him. The way the trees were large and mighty, still growing and bursting with beautiful, luscious green leaves that danced in the breeze. How the birds could sing for hours on end and never change their tune. The way the light bounced off of the water and broke into a million pieces, reflecting across the small waves that moved the boat. Nature was all too incredible to him.

Emery watched Gryffin on the other side of the boat. His eyes wandered throughout their surroundings. Like a child in a candy store, he didn't linger on one thing for too long. It was as if Gryffin had never seen this place before. He had though. Many times before, Gryffin had come with his father in a canoe and fished in this exact spot. Maybe that was why he loved it so much; it reminded him of his father. Emery still couldn't understand why this was a crucial part to making her a more positive person.

The boat rocked steadily back and forth as the small waves passed under them. Gryffin finally fixed his gaze back to Emery. He could see that she was not at all enjoying herself. She was bored. Gryffin decided to try another tactic. "Isn't it crazy how all of this is here?"

"What do you mean?"

"I mean, look around you. Look at all of this incredible land-scape, the puffy clouds in the sky. Isn't it crazy how you can get so caught up in the bustle of the city that you forget that this is what is looked like before the buildings went up?" Gryffin leaned back in the boat and looked up deep into the sky. "Life is everywhere, Emery. In the grass, in the leaves on the trees, the fish swimming around us." He dipped his hand into the cool water. "This is how we all started. From scratch."

Emery processed what Gryffin had said. She thought it made complete sense. On top of that, he was poetic and insightful about the whole subject. Emery made a note of that. She took another look around her. Emery could not deny it was beautiful. Once she really thought about it, she realized how the earth itself was a living thing. Breathing and coursing with life everywhere, even in places that were overlooked. Places like this.

The wind brushed passed her face, soaking up into her nostrils and giving her a clean and refreshed feeling. She could see what Gryffin meant now. But she really didn't want to admit that to him. So Emery settled on saying, "It is peaceful out here."

"Yeah, it is." Gryffin smoothed his hand through the water. "It's a great place to clear your head after the city has filled it up with so many fumes."

"Is that why you like it so much?"

"Well, that and it's kind of a place that holds some memories. My father would take me fishing here as a kid all the time."

Emery found that sweet. "That's nice. It's a great place to fish."

"Yeah," Gryffin said absently.

His mind went back to when he and his father went out in their small wooden boat. He always had to wear an uncomfortable racer-red life jacket and be careful not to tip the boat. Gryffin was a bit clumsy as a child. One time he did fall out of the boat. He remembered the fear as he plunged overboard, how it felt when he tried taking a gasp of air but only retained water. The way the light looked from under the water—big, white, and unattainable. Seconds after Gryffin was underwater, his father was next to him, pulling him with strong arms to the surface.

"Careful, buddy," his father said after they had both gotten back into the boat. "The fish like to nibble on worms, not little boys." His father smiled at him and gave him a bear hug. That was when Gryffin knew he wanted to be like his father. Noble and caring.

Emery's voice snapped Gryffin back to reality. "Do you still fish with him?" she asked.

The muscles in Gryffin's jaw tensed. "No, not anymore. He died a few years ago." He did not want to sound morbid or bring

Emery down. The whole point of this trip was to lift her spirit a little. Gryffin gave her a half smile. "He would have liked you."

"Why's that?"

"You're tough. You don't let people push you around."

Emery smiled to herself. He thought she was tough. Was that a good sign? Wait, why did she even care? Emery pulled herself back from her thoughts and decided to ease the conversation, "It's nice here. I like it."

Gryffin wore a satisfied grin.

"Thank you for showing me this, Gryffin."

"You're welcome." Excitement instantly replaced his satisfaction. "Wait, does that mean it worked?"

"Yes, it worked," she said softly.

"I'm sorry. What was that, Miss Everett?" He put his hand to his ear like he couldn't hear her.

Emery sighed and said more loudly, "Yes, it worked, Gryffin. Everything out here is truly lovely." She hated to admit it, but it honestly felt good to.

Gryffin retrieved the list from his pocket along with a pen he had also been storing. He unfolded the paper and crossed what Emery assumed was the first task off. "Yes! Step one, completed." Gryffin spared no expense at being happy for his achievement.

"Okay, okay, you got me." Emery shook her head at his excitement. She laughed to herself, enjoying every moment of it. "What's next on your list?"

Gryffin stopped shuffling the paper back into its folded position. He wore a look of surprise. "You want to keep doing it?"

"Yeah." Emery shrugged. "Seems like you have a good thing going here. And I don't have much else going on right now."

That huge smile Emery had seen a couple times before appeared back on Gryffin's face. "Okay." He finished folding the list and put both it and the pen back in his pocket. "You'll find out what number two on the list is tomorrow." Gryffin gave her a cryptic grin like he was up to something.

Emery raised her eyebrows. "That is how you're going to play it?"

"Yep." Gryffin's grin went from being mysterious to cheesy. Emery couldn't help but adore it. "Do you want to head back?"

"Not yet." Emery watched as the wind blew through the trees, shaking the leaves and making a soft rustling sound. "Can we stay here a little longer?"

Gryffin nodded. "As long as you need."

The two did not talk for the remainder of their time out in the little boat as they floated in the middle of the pond. They sat comfortably in silence, the rustling and babbling of the life around them filling the void. Emery basked in the sun, absorbing its heat and light. She decided that she didn't completely hate this place as she did most places. Emery could bear the outdoors in this little boat—that is, as long as Gryffin was there to bear it with her.

Chapter 6

*E*mery could barely focus at work the next morning. Her mind kept drifting back to her time with Gryffin yesterday. After being outside for a little while that afternoon, she couldn't help but feel cooped up in her small office now. She wanted to breathe the fresh air again and run her fingers through the water. Emery then realized that Gryffin's first task really did work. She wouldn't tell him that though. Emery took no chances. When her mind was set on something, there was no changing it. Even if Emery was wrong, she wouldn't acknowledge it; she would simply switch the subject or ignore the matter altogether. Some would say that this was a sure sign of an inflated ego. But in Emery's case, it prevented her from being vulnerable, from showing any hint of insecurity whatsoever. It was a way to protect herself from heartache.

The day went by slowly, dragging with every tick of the clock that hung on the wall. Her office didn't help much either. It was bland and dull colored, and no signs of personal effects were to be seen. A desk, a chair, a file cabinet, a clock, and a computer were all Emery needed to make this space hers. She tapped her pen on her desk, watching the minute hand slowly move forward. Emery wondered what was next on Gryffin's list. What would they be doing this evening? She couldn't believe she was actually looking forward to spending time outside of her daily routine with someone she barely knew. This was absurd behavior for Emery, and she didn't quite know how to feel about it. She waited impatiently for the clock to strike five so she could meet her mysterious friend and go on another escapade with him.

At about four forty-five, Emery's cell phone buzzed on her desk. She looked at the caller ID before answering. There was no name, just a number she didn't recognize. Thinking it might be a client, Emery cleared her throat and accepted the incoming call.

"Hello, this is Emery Everett," she greeted professionally.

"Miss Everett," a familiar voice said, "you sound so different when you're on the clock."

"Gryffin, I wasn't expecting you to call." Emery had forgotten she had given him her number in the park yesterday.

"I assumed as much." Gryffin sounded like he was smiling. "So are we still on for today?"

"I was planning on it," Emery replied.

"Good." Gryffin sounded more excited now. "I'll pick you up at five thirty. We have a little bit of a drive before we can cross off our next task."

"Okay, I'll text you my address. Where are we going?" Emery disliked surprises.

"Trust me, you'll love it," Gryffin reassured her.

Emery sighed, seeing no point in pestering him for answers. "Okay, fine."

"Awesome. Oh! Make sure you wear something comfy and with layers," he added.

"If you say so."

"I'll see you soon, Miss Everett." Gryffin chuckled.

"See you," Emery said and then hung up. She didn't know where Gryffin was taking her or what they were going to be doing, but truthfully, she was a little excited.

Gryffin pulled up to a tall apartment building near The Lift. He parked his small red car along the curb and turned off the engine. *Just take a deep breath, Gryff. She's just a girl.* He was focused on not making a fool of himself in front of Emery. Gryffin took a deep breath and got out of his car. He walked up to the door and looked for Emery's name on the call list. Sure enough, he found *Emery Everett Apt 32* toward the bottom of the list. Gryffin pressed the button that buzzed her room. He took a step back as he waited for her to come down. Why was he so nervous? This was so strange to him. He had never experienced this feeling on stage or anywhere in his life. So why was he feeling anxious?

Then Gryffin knew why.

The front door opened, and out stepped Emery. She was wearing light blue jeans and a dark gray sweatshirt with a decent-sized light gray purse swung over her shoulder. Her long, dark hair was pulled up into a loose ponytail, showing that she didn't have much time to mess with it before Gryffin arrived.

Emery smiled as she shut the door behind her. Gryffin couldn't control his muscles to smile back; he just stared at her. He couldn't help it; she was beautiful. Even in casual clothes and not the office wear he had seen her in the other night. Emery's bright eyes ignited something in Gryffin, a sense of passion. Gryffin had never felt this way before. He wanted to make Emery smile and laugh. He wanted to be someone she could trust. Even if she wasn't interested in him like he was in her, Gryffin could settle with being her friend. There was no way he could see his life without her now that she was in it.

"Gryffin? You awake in there?" Emery waved her hand in front of his face.

"Hm? Yeah, I'm awake." Gryffin blushed a little, embarrassed that she noticed his gaze upon her. "Sorry, my mind was just wandering."

"Sorry to keep you waiting."

"No, you're fine." Gryffin smiled. "Shall we?" He motioned to his car.

"If we must," Emery said with that sarcasm Gryffin loved.

To Emery's surprise, Gryffin opened the door for her and even shut it after she was settled into her seat. *Chivalry isn't extinct after all.* If he was trying to impress her, he was doing a decent job so far. Gryffin got into the driver's side and plopped down into his seat. He buckled himself in and started up the car.

The drive was quiet at first. Emery watched the blurred trees as they passed outside the window. Gryffin kept glancing over to see if Emery was uncomfortable with the silence. To his surprise, she wasn't. There was a hint of a smile on her face as she watched nature pass them by outside the car. She liked car rides; she liked the feeling of going somewhere. Seeing that she was content, he didn't strike up any conversation with her. At the same time, Gryffin did not like the silence. Maybe Emery wouldn't mind if he put on some music.

"Do you mind if I?" Gryffin pointed to the car radio.

Emery shook her head, "No, go ahead."

Gryffin pressed the power button on the small stereo system. He scanned through the channels, waiting for something to catch his interest. "Do you want to listen to anything specific?" He wasn't sure if she had a certain style she liked to listen to. He guessed her to be a pop or electronic kind of girl.

"No, nothing in particular," she replied.

Gryffin decided to switch to the CD player setting. One of his favorite bands flowed through the speakers. Their song was smooth and vibrant. Gryffin noticed Emery's foot tapping along to the beat and her head nodding with the melody.

"Have you ever been to a concert?" Gryffin asked.

"Just the live bands Friday nights at the Lift," Emery answered.

"So you've never seen any big-name bands play before?"

"No." Emery shook her head.

Gryffin looked shocked. "Well, why not?"

"I don't know. I guess I've never thought about it, and I don't have a favorite artist to go see."

Gryffin took a long look at her like he didn't understand what she was saying. "I am so disappointed. How can you not have a favorite band or artist?"

"Music isn't a huge part of my life. I like it, but I don't surround myself with it," Emery said honestly.

"Why?"

Emery shrugged. "I suppose some people cope with music, and I just find something else to do. I like music. I think it's inspiring and fun, but I don't ever take the time to actually sit down and listen to it."

"Fair enough." She did have a point; not everyone turned to music. "So, instead of listening to music, what do you do to let steam off or relax after a long day?"

"I work." Emery looked back to her window. "And if I have no work to do, I find it."

"That doesn't sound relaxing at all," Gryffin said.

Emery chuckled. "No, I suppose it doesn't."

"Well, listen to this song." Gryffin skipped to track four on the CD. "Just let your mind wander and take in the lyrics."

"Music is really your life, isn't it?" Emery sighed.

"Well, it's gotten me through a lot. Now listen." He nodded to the speaker.

Emery sat back in her seat to get more comfortable. The song started off with a guitar riff, no drums or percussion. The melody kicked in, and the singer began. A man with a suave not-too-deep voice sang quietly along to the tune. From what Emery gathered, the song was about being in a big city full of people but at the same time feeling alone. She liked the way it sounded, easy and flowing … like a steady stream or a meadow. This made her think of the pond that she and Gryffin were at yesterday. Emery slowly looked over to Gryffin, who was looking straight ahead. He was tapping his thumb on the steering wheel. Emery watched him and how he let the music take him on some distant journey in his heart. No one had ever taken such an interest in Emery before. She didn't understand why Gryffin was so keen on being her friend, but she wasn't about to question it. Gryffin was different from other people. He was not afraid to live and be passionate about something. Most people were only passionate about themselves.

Emery and Gryffin caught each other's eyes. Gryffin simply smiled at her, and Emery smiled back. She returned to looking out the window, as she had before, but she thought about Gryffin the rest of the trip.

Chapter 7

"**O**kay, we're here," Gryffin said as he put the gear in park. He swiftly got out of his car and jogged over to the passenger side where he opened the door for Emery. Emery stepped out of Gryffin's car and took in her surroundings. From what she could tell, Gryffin had taken her to a carnival outside of their small town. She had seen posters up around The Lift the past month for some type of festival taking place a couple of towns over; this must have been what was being advertised.

"So," Gryffin said as he shut Emery's car door, "what do you think?"

Emery wasn't sure what to think, so she settled on stating the obvious. "You brought me to a carnival."

"Not a carnival so much as a festival," Gryffin corrected her. "It's the annual fair at the end of the summer, full of rides, games, and elephant ears to your heart's content."

"And the point of this is?" Emery didn't much care for being in a crowd of people.

Gryffin placed his hands on her shoulders and spoke slowly as if to make sure she understood him. "To have some fun."

Emery replied with her infamous eye roll. Gryffin took that as the sign to proceed to the fairgrounds.

The ticket line was long but moved quickly. The two older ladies in the ticket booth were pleasant but also stuck to business to help the line move along. When they were next in line, Gryffin took a step ahead of Emery to pay for his ticket. Emery rummaged through her purse to find her wallet. When Gryffin saw this, he put a hand up to stop her and said, "No, I got this one."

"I can buy my own ticket, Gryffin." Emery pulled out her small wallet and flipped through some cash.

"I know you can, but I would like to buy your ticket. Besides, it's my list, and I'll take responsibility for any costs it might entail."

Emery narrowed her eyes at Gryffin, unsure of what he was up to. Gryffin just looked at her with raised eyebrows, letting Emery know that he wasn't going to back off of this one. Seeing no point in arguing with him, she sighed and agreed to let him pay.

"Two please," Gryffin said to one of the ladies in the ticket booth as he pushed a twenty-dollar bill across the counter. The woman took his money and made change. Then she gave him two wristbands. Gryffin thanked her and handed one of the wristbands to Emery. They fastened their neon-green bands onto their wrists and walked through the front gate of the festival.

Emery and Gryffin walked around the fairground for a few minutes, taking in the atmosphere. Families, couples, and groups of teenagers passed them, all smiling and having a seemingly great time. Emery was not fond of this place, mainly because she wasn't fond of people. Gryffin smelled the fair food and was instantly enthralled by the lively fair environment. He was loving every moment as memories of being a child and going on rides with his brother swept into his mind. Although maybe he was enjoying it more with Emery there ...

"So, where to first?" Gryffin asked. "You have the tilt-a-whirl over there, the rickety roller coaster over there that looks more like a safety hazard, the big swings, and the ever-popular Ferris wheel. What'll it be, Miss Everett?"

Emery looked from the tilt-a-whirl to the red roller coaster and then back to Gryffin. "I'm not much of a ride girl, Gryffin."

"I figured as much." Gryffin had a plan already. He pointed to a small child's roller coaster that got barely ten feet off the ground. "Then we'll start you off small."

"A kiddie coaster? Really?" She raised an eyebrow.

"Come on. We'll work you up to the big swings." Gryffin winked. He began to make his way to the line for the kiddie ride. Emery huffed when she thought he was out of hearing distance and then proceeded to follow him.

Gryffin and Emery looked like giants standing in line for the kiddy roller coaster. Among all of the children ten and under, they were the only adults to be seen. Emery could not believe she was doing this. She even thought about making an excuse like she wasn't feeling well to get out of riding this sad excuse for a roller coaster. But she saw the glee in Gryffin's eyes and decided to suck it up. Normally, Emery would just bluntly say no to something if she didn't want to do it, but with Gryffin she couldn't find the heart to. He had a way of making the most ridiculous, stupid things look appealing. Maybe that was why this whole list thing was working out. Or could it be that she just really liked spending time with Gryffin? Emery pushed the thought into the back of her mind. There was no way she would fall for Gryffin. She couldn't. Right?

The rocket-red, six-passenger car for the kiddie coaster came back to the beginning of the track and stopped with a harsh clank. The children in the car unfastened their seat belts, and the ride operator unlatched each of their lap bars. After all of the riders had made their way to the exit gate, the operator allowed the next six in line to get on the coaster. Emery and Gryffin were third and fourth in line, so it was their turn. When they reached the front of the line to get to their seat, the line operator stopped them.

"Excuse me," she said with her hand out, "you can't get on this ride."

"Why not?" Gryffin asked.

"Because you're both too big. There's a height and age limit. I'm pretty sure neither of you are twelve." She looked from Gryffin to Emery inquisitively.

"Look, I just wanted to start my friend out on a smaller coaster before we ride the bigger rides," Gryffin explained. "Please, could you just let us on this one time?"

"It's not my call. I'm just following the rules." The ride operator shrugged.

A look of disappointment took Gryffin's face. Emery saw this and felt bad for him. She said, "What if we were riding with a kid? Could we get on then?" What was she doing?

The ride operator nodded. "Yeah, but you don't have a kid, do you?"

Gryffin smiled and quickly turned to the line of anxious kids waiting to get in line. He disappeared for a moment and returned with a young girl and boy. The little girl, who looked to be seven, had light brown hair that was pulled into pigtails. The little boy, who Emery presumed was the little girl's brother, looked roughly eight and sported tiger face-paint. "Yes we do." Gryffin motioned to them.

"We do?" Emery looked at the two children who were smiling at her cheerfully.

"Yes, this is Kyle and Samantha," Gryffin said. "They're scared to go by themselves." Kyle and Samantha nodded as if they had rehearsed it together. Whatever Gryffin's plan was, it seemed to be working, "So, can we go?"

The ride operator eyed the four of them for a moment, unsure if she should buy into their tall tale. "Go ahead." She stepped aside to let them through.

"Great! Let's do this, guys!" Gryffin clapped his hands and motioned for everyone to follow him. The two kids whooped and ran inside. Emery thanked the ride operator and entered the kiddie coaster.

Gryffin sat with Kyle in the seats behind Samantha and Emery. Emery turned back to Gryffin. "How did you get these kids to come with us?"

"With charm and wit." Gryffin winked.

"We're still getting our five dollars, right?" Kyle asked from beside him. Gryffin darted a look to Kyle, who giggled at him.

Emery saw it all clearly now and chuckled. "All class." Gryffin blushed a little, knowing he would never hear the end of this.

"Excuse me." The young girl tugged on Emery's shirtsleeve. "Can you help me?" She held up one of the buckle straps.

Emery had never been good with children. She was awkward around them, not knowing how to act or what to say to them. Emery had never thought, *I want kids someday.* Being responsible for someone's life, raising them the right way—it was all too much pressure for her.

Samantha waited for Emery to respond. "Sure," Emery slowly agreed. She took the strap from the little girl and the other strap that was on her side. She clasped them together with the buckle on her strap. The belt was a bit loose on them from the previous riders, so Emery reached around to the other side to pull the access strap to tighten the belt up.

"Hey. that tickles!" The little girl giggled as Emery felt for the end of the belt, which was lying by Samantha's stomach.

"Oh, I'm sorry!" she apologized.

"It's okay." Samantha grinned.

"Do you want to pull on that end for me to tighten the belt up a little bit?" Emery didn't want to cause any more discomfort for the child.

"Mm-hm." Samantha took the end of the strap and pulled. Small veins popped out of her neck as if she was doing this with all of her tiny might.

Emery chuckled. "Whoa, look how strong you are!".

When Samantha decided she was done tightening the strap, she turned to Emery and exclaimed, "You should see me throw a baseball! I can throw it farther than Kyle!"

"Nuh-uh!" Kyle protested from behind. "I was just sick that day!"

Gryffin laughed at the siblings arguing. When they were through, Gryffin watched Emery and Samantha talk together.

Emery was a natural with kids; Gryffin admired that about her. She carried on a conversation with this little girl about hair ties and even tee ball. He smiled, enjoying the innocence of the child.

The ride operator came around to each individual pair of riders and checked their seat belts and then lowered their lap bars, locking them into place. She went back to the operating system and spoke into the microphone. "Riders, ready?

"Yes!" they yelled. Emery felt their excitement and even yelled too. Gryffin laughed, surprised that Emery was so into this.

"Okay, here we go!" The ride operator turned a key and pushed a red button, and the car was off.

As the coaster car began to move toward the first hill with a whopping drop of eight feet, Gryffin began to pretend like he was scared to make Kyle laugh. He pretended to try to get out of the seat and covered his eyes with his hands, asking Kyle to tell him when it was all over. Kyle was laughing his head off, and his little giggle made Emery laugh too. When they reached the top of the hill, Samantha grabbed Emery's arm and held it tight, burying her face in Emery's shoulder. Emery she put her arm around the little girl to comfort her. She wasn't sure what else to do, so she simply said, "It's okay. It's just a little hill." Emery tried to reassure her. "You know you're going to miss the ride if you keep your eyes closed." The little girl didn't budge. Emery decided to take a different approach. "Kyle has his eyes opened. I thought you were stronger than him."

This got Samantha's attention. "I am!" She snapped her head up.

"I thought so. Tell you what. I promise I will keep my eyes open if you will."

The little girl smiled and nodded. "Okay." She turned her head back to the hill.

Gryffin overheard all of this and realized that Emery wasn't so coldhearted after all. There was some hope for her to see a brighter side of things. This was more proof that the list was working.

The kiddie coaster reached the top of the first hill, and all of the kids screamed at the top of their lungs. Gryffin did the same, hoping it would make Samantha laugh. He succeeded, getting not only her to chuckle but also Emery and all of the other kids. Gryffin exaggerated the entire ride, flailing his arms and yelling for Kyle to protect him. All of the riders cheered and giggled the whole way through the one-minute ride. When the car came to a stop, Gryffin sank down into his seat like he was overcome with relief.

"I kept my eyes open!" Samantha cheered.

"I know! You were awesome! You were even stronger than my friend!" Emery boosted her up even more.

"He was crying for his momma!" Samantha pointed and laughed.

Gryffin pouted and played along. "Hey! It was a scary ride!" He looked to Kyle. "Right?"

Kyle shook his head, giggling.

"What! You're on their side?" Gryffin acted shocked. He tickled Kyle's belly. "I thought we were bros!" Kyle laughed even harder and tried to swat Gryffin's hands away.

The ride operator unlocked the lap bars and said everyone was okay to exit the car. Emery and Gryffin unbuckled their belt straps and helped the kids out of the car. They all walked to the exit gate, and Samantha held Emery's hand the whole way. After they went through the gate, it was time for the four of them to part ways.

"Thanks for riding with us, guys," Emery said.

"Mm-hm!" To Emery's surprise, Samantha jumped up and hugged her. Emery awkwardly wrapped her arms around the little girl and hugged her back.

"Thanks for keeping your eyes open," Samantha whispered.

Emery smiled. "Any time." Samantha let go of Emery and took her brother's hand.

"Oh." Gryffin realized he had forgotten to give them money. "Here's your five bucks, little man." He handed a five-dollar bill to Kyle. "And for you as well." He gave Samantha one too. "Have fun, you two. Stay out of trouble, okay?"

Kyle and Samantha grinned and skipped away. Gryffin and Emery watched them go, knowing they would never forget their time with them.

"So what did you think?" Gryffin asked as they began to walk again.

"I thought it was ..." Emery searched for the right word. "Fun."

"Really? *You* had *fun*? I am just ... wow." Gryffin put his hand on his chest in bewilderment.

"What?" Emery was uncomfortable with this look.

"You're smiling. Actually smiling," he said.

Emery didn't realize this; she couldn't help it. "So?"

"So, that was the point of this whole trip. To get you to have some fun, to let loose."

"Okay, so it worked. Are you happy?" There was no way of hiding how much she was enjoying herself.

"Fervently." He nodded. "Now onto the big swings!" He pointed and began to run in the direction of the ride.

"Wait, what?" Emery didn't realize that she had agreed to the next step. *What have I gotten myself into?* She shook her head and picked up the pace to follow Gryffin.

The lights on the food stands and carnival rides glistened in the night. Bright red, blue, yellow, and neon lights reflected off the metal rides and throughout the park. It was truly a beautiful sight. Emery and Gryffin had ridden six rides, including the rickety coaster, and had successfully finished an elephant ear and a few hot dogs. The night was coming to a close for them, and neither of them wanted it to. They made their way to the front gate with the rest of the visitors as the festival was coming to a close. As they walked out the front gate, Gryffin pulled Emery aside and began leading her along the side of the fairgrounds.

"Where are we going?" Emery asked as she followed Gryffin through the darkened lot.

"There's one more place I want to go before we leave," Gryffin answered. They walked until they reached a small hill a decent distance away from the festival. "Come on." Gryffin held out his hand. Emery hesitated, not one to openly receive help from anyone for anything. But she had come this far and done this much, so she took it.

A small hint of warmth flowed through Gryffin as he held her hand and led her up the hill. When they reached the top, they sat down and looked over the fairgrounds in front of them. The lights one by one at the festival began to go out as they were shutting down the rides and the various stands.

Emery liked watching the lights dim and then go to black. She wondered if this was what Gryffin had wanted to show her.

"My brother and I used to come here all the time," Gryffin said, watching the festival ahead of them die down. "We would come up here to watch the lights go out at the end of the night. It was kind of a tradition."

"You and your brother are pretty close then?"

"Yeah, we were when we were younger. But things change, you know?" He seemed bothered by this.

"Do you not see each other anymore?" Emery asked.

"Not often, no. And when we do, it turns into an argument."

"Oh." Emery felt like she had pried.

"What about you?" Gryffin shifted the subject. "Do you have any siblings?"

Emery shook her head. "No, just me and my mom."

"Ah, only child. That makes sense." Gryffin seemed to have unraveled something about Emery.

"What's that supposed to mean?"

"I saw how you were with Samantha back there. At first you were really uncomfortable and unsure of yourself. If you had a brother or sister, you wouldn't be so stiff," Gryffin explained.

This did make sense to Emery. "I supposed that's true."

"Once you talked to her though, you were a natural. You're really good with kids."

The thought of Emery with kids made her laugh, "That's a no. I'm awful with kids." She chuckled nervously.

"Really, you're not. You just have to warm up to them first, and once you do, it's like everything comes naturally to you. She really liked you, Miss Everett."

"You don't have to call me that," Emery said.

"What?"

"Miss Everett. You don't have to call me that. You can just call me Emery." She wondered why he called her by her last name. Only Gryffin had ever called her that, and she actually didn't mind it. She didn't want Gryffin to know that she had grown fond of it though.

"I know," Gryffin said, and Emery was okay with it. "Are you close with your mother?" Gryffin decided to take a chance and see if Emery would reveal more about herself.

"We were." Emery tensed a little at the question.

"Do you mind if I ask what happened?"

Emery's jaw tightened for a moment. "She died. A long time ago."

"I'm sorry." Gryffin felt awful for bringing up a sensitive subject.

"It's okay. You didn't know," Emery said.

"I guess we have something in common," Gryffin said. Emery cocked her head to the side as if she didn't understand what he meant. Gryffin continued, "We both lost our parents too soon."

Emery tightened her jaw again; seeing the vulnerability in Gryffin's eyes made her feel uncomfortable. She didn't want to open up to him any more; she knew better than that. Emery straightened up and took a small breath. "It's pretty here at night."

"Yeah, it is," Gryffin agreed. But he wasn't looking at the festival. He couldn't take his eyes off of Emery. She was transfixed with the distinguishing lights of the festival, and she was oddly serene.

Gryffin noticed she had that same look when they were at the lake, as if she had never experienced something so simple and yet so elegant before. He didn't want to stop watching her. He couldn't. Emery was beautiful, even more so like this and when she smiled, which was a rare sight.

Emery felt Gryffin's stare upon her. She tried to ignore it at first, thinking he would go back to watching the festival close down as she was doing now. He didn't. Emery slowly glanced over to Gryffin to see if her feeling was correct. It was. Even when their eyes met, he didn't look away like he was embarrassed that she had caught him. Instead, Gryffin kept his gaze on her, wearing that small, half smile. His eyes were pulling her in, making her feel something deep inside herself that she had never felt. What was it? Warmth? No, it couldn't be, and Emery didn't want to find out. She cleared her throat, snapping Gryffin from his trance. "It's getting late. I should probably get back," Emery said.

"Yeah, of course." Gryffin's attempt at having a moment with Emery had failed. He stood and offered to help Emery up, but by the time he did, she was already on her feet. They walked down the hill and back to the empty parking lot in silence. When they reached the car, Gryffin unlocked it and opened Emery's door as he had done before. The ride home was quiet again, except for the CD that was still playing from the ride up. Emery enjoyed the music and the silence with Gryffin. It was comfortable and easy, something she could get used to. Gryffin tapped along to the songs and occasionally glanced over at Emery. Emery knew he did this; she could see his reflection in the window as she looked outside. She smiled every time he did.

Later that night, after Gryffin dropped Emery at her apartment and made sure she made it in safely, he returned home and plopped down on his bed. He took out the list from his wallet and checked off the second item. Gryffin then drifted off to sleep with the list lying on his chest and a smile on his face.

Chapter 8

The next few weeks consisted of Emery and Gryffin crossing off things from the infamous list. One day the two went to an old movie, something in black and white that Emery had never heard of. She was hesitant to go at first because she was a stickler for certain types of movies. But Gryffin persuaded her yet again to give it a chance. To her surprise, she enjoyed the film and even asked Gryffin if they could return to watch another soon.

Another item they crossed off was setting off fireworks. Gryffin wouldn't tell Emery the purpose of this exercise when asked what the point was. They drove out to an abandoned lot with no houses around. It was in the middle of nowhere where they couldn't disturb anyone or be disturbed themselves. The sun was setting quickly, forcing Gryffin to get the first set of fireworks ready to go. He lit the fuse to the first firework and ran to Emery, who was standing a good distance away from the flaming firetrap. The firework rocketed into the sky just as Gryffin reached Emery.

It shot off high in the orange and red painted sky, crackling and flashing bright blue as it reached the point of breaking. Emery was wrapped up in the beauty of the colors that flashed in the sky as each firework soared into the atmosphere. Her face beamed like a child on the Fourth of July as she pointed out the ones she liked the most. She and Gryffin even rated them on a scale of one to ten. Gryffin would purposely rate the worst ones the highest to get a rise out of Emery. He thought she was adorable when she got riled up. Emery knew he did it on purpose but played along.

When the fireworks were all shot off, Gryffin broke out the sparklers. He lit Emery's first and then his. They ran through the darkness of the night swinging their sparks of light through the air carelessly and aimlessly. Gryffin chased Emery through the lot and around his car with a sparkler in hand. Emery laughed until her sides hurt, and her chest heaved as she tried to catch a breath from the laughter and the running combined. After the last of the sparklers were lit, Gryffin and Emery lay on the hood of his car, watching the star-filled sky above them.

"May I guess what the reason for this was?" Emery asked as she stared into the darkened sky.

"You may." Gryffin allowed her to put the pieces together.

Emery was quiet for a moment, putting her theory together. "Well, I think the reason for this item on your list was to show me that it's okay to still be a kid."

"Meaning …" Gryffin waited for more.

"Meaning," Emery continued, "I don't have to take everything so seriously. Sometimes, you need to look through the eyes of a child to see things for their true worth. Like we did when we were young."

Gryffin turned his head, an impressed look on his face. "Very good, Miss Everett."

"Thank you," Emery said, pleased with herself.

"But that's not the reason behind this exercise." Gryffin let that sink in.

"Oh." Emery was confused. "You said that I was right though."

"No, I said you did well on trying to figure it out. I never said you were right."

Emery turned to face him. "What was the meaning then? Hm?" She spoke as if her reasoning was superior to whatever his was.

Gryffin took the challenge. "You know how whenever you see a firework, it doesn't end with just one?" He spoke with wisdom, something that caught Emery off guard. "There are always more to follow—each firework bursting with its own color and light but always right behind another one. That's how acts work. One act from one person follows another. Good or bad, a chain reaction gets set off every single time. Can you imagine if everyone set off a reaction by doing something good? The world would be so much more inviting. People wouldn't be unhappy all the time, and friendship and loyalty would be strong within every living person."

Emery had no words for Gryffin. She just stared at him in astonishment. How did this fun-loving, kidlike man think such deep thoughts? Emery was impressed by his knowledge and wisdom. She also noted his seemingly endless chivalry and fight for the greater good. No one else thought like he did. No one else acted like he did. Maybe that was why she was so fond of Gryffin. He was like no one she had ever met before. Gryffin made her see everything differently. He made her question herself, her beliefs, what was right and wrong, what really should matter in life. Gryffin was like no other.

"You could say the reason behind what we did tonight was to show you that you can make a difference. There's always someone watching and waiting to be inspired, to be set off. You can be that inspiration, Miss Everett. We all can. You have the power to make a difference," Gryffin concluded.

"Thank you," Emery said after a few quiet moments.

"For what?" Gryffin asked.

"For being you."

Gryffin smiled at her with a broad grin. Emery smiled back. This was something Gryffin had seen only once in a while. As time passed and they spent more time together, Emery's smile steadily became more constant. Gryffin saw to it that she would never go back to that somber guise that she had grown accustomed to. He loved her smile, and he loved that she was smiling for him even more.

Next on the list was to watch the sunrise. So Gryffin and Emery met at four thirty in the morning at the same park where they had completed their first task together. Emery groggily and lazily walked over to the bench near the pond. She dragged her feet the whole way, not thrilled to be there at that hour. This time, it was Gryffin who waited for Emery at the bench. He was dead tired too, but he masked it well with a big grin and a lot of caffeine beforehand.

"Good morning, Miss Everett." Gryffin nodded to her and stood up.

"Please." She put her hand up to stop him. "It's too early for pleasantries." She slumped onto the park bench.

Sporting sweatpants and a hoodie, Emery couldn't have cared less about looking good that early in the morning. Gryffin, however, looked cleaned up even at the crack of dawn, even if it was just jeans and a T-shirt he was wearing. He didn't comb his hair before coming to the park, so he wore a red baseball cap backwards on his head to hide his messy mop of blond hair. Gryffin realized Emery was not a morning person. Even with her hair up in a messy bun and her sweatshirt being oversized, Gryffin still thought she was nothing short of lovely.

"The sun will be up soon," Gryffin reassured her.

Emery sighed. "What's the point of this one, Gryffin? Another lesson about enjoying the beauty of nature?" Emery said with a snarky tone.

"No," Gryffin replied. "Just the feeling of being awake before the world."

Emery rolled her eyes, uninterested in his deep words today. "Whatever you say." She rubbed the sleep of her eyes as a yawn escaped her mouth.

"Not used to being up this early, are we, Miss Everett?" Gryffin teased.

Emery stuck out her tongue at him. "I'm sorry I'm not a robot, which is the only logical explanation as to how you are so awake right now."

"I'm not the coldhearted one here," Gryffin poked.

"Har-har-har." Emery crossed her arms as if she was offended.

Gryffin chuckled. Emery smiled and shook her head, knowing it was all in good fun.

"Can I ask you something?" Gryffin said.

"You just did," Emery retorted.

"Okay, wise guy, you know what I mean."

"Sure."

Gryffin slid his body so that he was fully facing Emery. He didn't look at her at first, thinking of how to start off what he was going to ask her about. Then Gryffin and Emery's eyes met, and he said, "I know nothing about you, Miss Everett. I mean, I know you work for a real estate company, and I also know that you really hate pickles and music weekends at The Lift." He paused for a moment when Emery smirked at his observations, and then he continued with a more serious tone, "I want to know your story, Miss Everett. Can you tell me something deeper than the surface?"

The question was so straightforward that Emery was caught off guard. Her first thought was to say that she didn't want to talk about it. Something in the back of her head, something small but strong, was telling her not to do her normal avoidance of emotional connection but to open up and let some light in the darkened parts of her heart. It was saying just three words: *let him in*. Emery struggled with this voice; a battle went on internally. Emery finally came to terms with what she needed to say to Gryffin. She took a breath and simply said, "There are a lot of things that happened to me that I don't talk about, Gryffin."

"Oh." Gryffin felt embarrassed that he had overstepped his boundaries.

"Don't take it personally, okay? I don't talk to people. I never have. So you asking me that is like asking me to jump off a cliff with no bungee cord."

"Why don't you open up to anyone?" Gryffin wanted to at least get a little deeper into the conversation.

Emery shrugged. "Because I always get hurt. And I can't take another hit like that again." Emery was not going to allow Gryffin to get more out of her than he already had. She turned her eyes back to the pond, waiting for the sun to rise.

"Will you promise me something then?" Gryffin hadn't looked back to the sky yet. His eyes were fixed on Emery. He leaned toward her. "If you ever get the urge to talk about anything, will you tell me first?"

Emery shot a playful grin to Gryffin. "I guess you'll have to find out."

Gryffin threw up his hands overdramatically. "What does that even mean?"

"You tell me. You're the one with the deep, meaningful list in your pocket." Emery motioned to him.

She had him there. "Fine. I guess I will," Gryffin agreed.

Just then, the sun began to rise over the pond. The light rays bounced through the trees, shining through the brilliant green of the leaves hanging on them. It glistened in the water and warmed Gryffin and Emery's cheeks. The sky was colored in bright, radiant pinks, oranges, and reds. No clouds were seen, making the sun the complete center of attention. Emery and Gryffin sat and watched this in silence. The comfortable hush of the park loomed over them, and not even a bird was heard now. Emery understood what Gryffin meant then. There was an incredible feeling that overcame her, as if she were the only one in the entire world who was awake. This sunrise was for her. These colors in the morning sky were painted for her eyes to adore. For the first time, the roles changed. Emery looked at Gryffin when he wasn't looking at her. A small smile crept on her face as she saw how taken Gryffin was with the show the sun was putting on for them. Gryffin knew she was looking at him, but he didn't react. He let her continue to do this. Hopefully, he thought, she was starting to feel something for him too.

Chapter 9

Almost four weeks had passed since Emery met Gryffin at The Lift. For four weeks they had been steadily crossing off tasks on Gryffin's list of positive perspective enhancing. She still couldn't believe that she had said yes to his list in the first place. Emery thought over these things as she was getting ready for work. She showered and made a breakfast of orange juice and fresh fruit. As she ate, she read the morning paper, keeping up to date with the current events. Emery didn't much like the girly magazines most women read, such as fashion or home-decorating magazines. She would rather skim through the headlines in the local paper or read up on what was happening in the world online. This was part of her morning routine.

When Emery was finished eating her breakfast, she rinsed out her bowl and placed it in her dishwasher along with her spoon and glass. She then picked out an outfit to wear for the day and laid it out on the bed. As she brushed her long, dark hair, she thought about what Gryffin had asked her the other day. Emery did want to talk to him about herself. He was the only one she had ever thought about sharing anything with. Wait—what did that mean? Emery stopped her brush in midstroke. Did she like Gryffin? Well, yes, she liked him. She enjoyed his company and thought he was a decent guy. But did she care more about him than just a friend? This scared Emery. She couldn't get involved again, not after … him. Emery pulled back the collar of her bathrobe, revealing her collarbone and part of her shoulder. Just under her clavicle was a scar that ran about an inch in length along her bone. She traced it with her fingers, the memory of the scar's perpetrator hanging over it. Emery shuddered. She quickly straightened her bathrobe and took a good look at herself in the mirror.

"You made it this far, Emery. Don't fall back now," she told the mirrored version of herself. With that, Emery went back to combing her hair, brushing the thought of being with someone out of her mind for the time being.

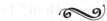

"So how's it going?" Derek asked. He plugged his guitar into the amp on the ground behind him. It was a few days before Escalates's next gig, and they wanted to get in as much practice as they could.

"What do you mean?" Gryffin strapped his guitar and slung it over his shoulder.

"With that girl, Emery." Derek spoke as if Gryffin knew exactly what he was talking about. "Aren't you guys still going out?"

"We aren't dating if that's what you're asking," Gryffin said, clearing the air.

"Whatever you want to call it, you guys are always together," Derek replied.

"Yeah, so?"

"Do you like her?"

"Are you talking about Emery?" Paige chimed in from behind her drum set. "You guys still together, Gryff?"

"Does everyone know about Emery?" Gryffin looked around.

"Well, now Alec does." Paige pointed her drumstick at the bassist.

"Who's Emery?" Alec said.

"Have you asked her out yet?" Derek asked.

"No," Gryffin answered.

"He basically has already. They do all these things that you would do on a date. That counts, right?"

"Who's Emery?" Alec said a little louder. The group dismissed his question.

"You gotta ask her out for real, Gryff," Derek stated. "Like, take her out to dinner or something. You know, keep it real classy."

"Who says I even want to ask her out?"

"Come on, it's obvious you like her." Paige twirled her drumsticks between her fingers.

"Yeah, even I can see that, bro." Derek sided with Paige.

Suddenly a loud C chord blared through the amp to their left. It shrilled and made the three musicians cover their ears. Their eyes all darted to Alec, who had cranked up his amplifier to high and strummed the note as loud as he could. Alec looked peeved as he asked for the final time, "Who is Emery!"

"Oh, this girl Gryffin loves," Paige answered for them as they took their hands off their ears.

"Whoa, now we're moving from like to love? Even I think that's a little fast for Gryffin," Derek said as he rubbed his ears. "Right?" He waited for Gryffin to ring in agreement.

Gryffin remained silent. This sparked all of Gryffin's bandmates' interests.

"Wait, wait." Alec walked closer to the group. "Do you love her?"

"I mean, I don't know." Gryffin shrugged. Paige and Derek's eyes widened. Gryffin scratched his head. "We've only known each other for a month now. I think I might be falling for her."

Derek leaned against his sound system. "Does she feel the same?"

"I don't know; it's hard to read her," Gryffin answered honestly. He was dumbfounded by how Emery's mind worked. That was one of the reasons he was so fond of her.

"You should talk to her," Paige said. "You won't ever know until you try."

Gryffin crossed his arms. "What if I make things weird? I like how we are right now, and I don't want that to change if I'm just nursing a crush on a girl who won't give me the time of day."

"She seems pretty fond of you. Look at how much time she spends with you. She wouldn't do that if she didn't like you a little," Paige pointed out.

"Maybe." Gryffin saw Paige's argument. "She's just so different from anyone I've ever met, you know? I know nothing personal about her; I don't even know her favorite color. I just don't think she's one of those girls to fall for anyone. She's strong. She doesn't need anyone." The room quieted down for a minute. It made sense to Gryffin now that he had said it out loud. Emery didn't *need* anyone. She was fine before Gryffin, and she would probably be fine after him. Still, a small part of him hoped that she did need him around.

"This may be a bad time to ask, but do you have those song lyrics finished?" Derek broke the silence.

"Actually, I do." Gryffin surprised the group.

"No kidding?" Alec chuckled. "And ironically not long after you met Emery either."

"Shut up," Gryffin joked. He turned up the volume on his guitar. "You guys remember the chords?" Gryffin ran a refresher course of the melody and the bass line along with the beat of the song. "Got it?"

Paige, Alec, and Derek all played along through the song once without the lyrics. After they had gotten a clean run-through, they decided to put the lyrics in. Gryffin cleared his throat and sang when he was supposed to. The song moved along smoothly, and the band members played it flawlessly. When the song was over, Gryffin took a deep breath as if he had just gotten something heavy off of his chest. He smiled to himself, pleased with his work. When he turned to hear the rest of the band's thoughts, he was surprised to see the three of them staring at him in awe.

"You need to ask out this girl." Derek patted his shoulder. "Because if she can get that out of you, I'm psyched to see what else you can come up with."

"Yeah, really good, Gryff." Alec nodded.

"You guys really think so?" Gryffin wasn't sure if they were ribbing him. It was a love song, after all, and the guys were known to pretend to be moved when he sang songs like this.

Paige stood up from her stool. "I think it's the best song you've written yet."

Gryffin nervously laughed. He wasn't used to all of the praise he was receiving. Was Emery really the reason he wrote such an amazing song? Was she his muse? Whatever she was to him, Gryffin wanted her to know. The band practiced the song at least four more times that day. Each time Gryffin sang it, he became more determined to talk to Emery.

Chapter 10

"Emery, look at me when I'm talking to you!" the man screamed in Emery's face. He stared down at her menacingly. His dark, unkempt hair and five o'clock shadow were evidence that he had not taken care of himself for a few days. He was drunk again. He was always drunk.

Emery remained calm and tried to keep her eyes from watering from the stench of alcohol on the man's breath as it ripped through her nostrils. She quietly said, "I'm sorry. I was going to take it out when I got home from work."

The man wagged his finger. "That's not what I asked, Em. I told you to take out the trash before you left last night. Now look at what you've done!" He pointed to the garbage can that lay on the kitchen floor. Some loose trash had escaped the bag and was scattered on the ground around it. "I ran right into it this morning, and now it's everywhere. If you would have taken care of it, I wouldn't have to pick up any of this crap!" The man huffed angrily.

"I'm sorry," Emery said. She saw no mercy in his eyes. "Do you think you could have taken it out though?" She knew asking this was a mistake, but she took the chance. "I had to work a double shift at the diner, and I didn't have time this morning before I left." Emery hoped he would see her side of things.

The man took a step back as if he were evaluating the situation. Then an uncomfortable smile crept onto his face. He took Emery's face in his hands and smoothly said, "I am the man of this house, and I will do what I think is in *our* best interest."

Something was still off with him. Emery felt an uneasy feeling in her chest as he stroked her cheeks with his thumbs. "I know," she agreed.

"So when I tell you to do something, like take out the trash," the man began, "you do it!" He slapped Emery right across the face. Emery fell a whole step back. Her cheek was pink from where he had hit her, and her head began to pound. She dare not let one tear loose; he would see that as an invitation to do more to her. He liked to beat up on her, or "teach her lessons" as he called it.

Emery slowly stood up, holding the side of her head with her hand. Rage was still enflamed in the man's eyes. She looked at him as composed as she could and said, "You're right. It won't happen again."

The man's expression softened, and a small hint of remorse took over him. He took Emery in his arms and held her. "You know I only do this for your benefit, right, Em? I love you. Please stop making me hurt you." He spoke softly.

Emery could hardly breathe for fear that she would begin to cry. She simply gave a small nod and hugged him back.

The alarm woke Emery from her slumber. She jolted at the sound, shooting up in bed. Emery quickly looked from side to side to make sure the man wasn't there. When she realized it was only a dream, Emery took a deep breath. Her eyes were wet, and she noticed small drops of water on her pillowcase as well. She must have been crying in her sleep again. It had been a long time since Emery had had a peaceful sleep. She had night terrors. Most of them were memories from a life before this one. Some of them were a mix of things that had happened, put into different scenarios that were even worse than what had originally happened. Either way, Emery woke up every morning either screaming or crying, never feeling rejuvenated from a good night's sleep.

Emery looked at her alarm clock. She had slept past her alarm; it had been going off for twenty minutes. *Great, I'm late.* Emery quickly got out of bed and put on the first thing she could find. Today, it was jeans and a light gray V-neck from on the top of the clothes she had gotten out of the dryer and had been too lazy to put away the night before. She combed quickly through her hair and then brushed her teeth. Gryffin would be there any minute to pick her up and take her to their next event. It was nine thirty, so she wondered where they had to be that early in the morning. But she knew if she asked, Gryffin would just reply, "You'll see," and Emery would roll her eyes and go along with it. Since they had been going through this list for a while now, she didn't mind the surprise anymore. It was actually more fun to her that way.

She heard the intercom buzz by the front door of her apartment. Emery rushed over and pushed the talk button. "I'll be right down!" She tried not to sound like she was still getting ready.

"Take your time." Gryffin's voice was cool.

Emery ran back to the bathroom and took one last look in the mirror. *This is as good as it's going to get.* She settled with her appearance and headed out the door.

Outside, Gryffin leaned against his car as he waited for Emery to come down. His mind raced with a million thoughts. The one that occurred the most was how he wanted to tell Emery how he felt about her. When it came down to it though, Gryffin was scared to. He had never been afraid of anything before this, so it was an odd feeling to have. All he knew was that he had to talk to Emery. He had to let her know what she meant to him before he lost his mind.

Emery finally exited her apartment building and was walking to Gryffin's car. Gryffin went around to the passenger's side and opened her door for her.

"You don't have to do that, you know," Emery said as she sat in the seat.

"As long as you're riding with me, it's going to happen." Gryffin smiled. "So you'd better get used to it." He closed her door. Emery chuckled. She could get used to this.

Gryffin got settled in the driver's seat and started up the car. He put it into drive, and they were off on their next endeavor. After a few moments of quiet, Gryffin said, "Well, aren't you going to ask where we are going?"

"No," Emery answered. "You'll just give me some enigmatic answer that basically means 'you'll never figure it out, so wait until we get there.'" Emery cocked an eyebrow teasingly.

"Am I that predictable?" Gryffin laughed. She was catching on to his evasive strategy.

"You are," she retorted.

"I better step up my game then if I want to keep my allure of mystery."

A ring sounded from Gryffin's jacket. He fumbled in his right pocket and pulled out his cell phone. Marcus's name appeared on the caller ID. "I'm sorry. I have to take this."

"No problem." Emery understood. She directed her attention out the window at the cars passing them so that she didn't appear to be eavesdropping.

"Hey, Marcus."

"Gryff, I need you." Marcus sounded shaky.

"I'm out with a friend right now. Can I pick you up in like an hour or something?" He really didn't want to deal with his junky brother right now.

"No, I need you now. Something happened, Gryff, and I need you to come home right now."

This got Gryffin worried. Marcus had never gone to his apartment without Gryffin taking him there. Why was he there now? Gryffin regretted what he was about to do. "Okay, yeah. Give me ten minutes."

"Please hurry."

Gryffin hung up the phone and pulled the car over to the side of the road and parked.

Emery said, "Is everything okay?"

"I'm sure it probably is, but my brother, Marcus, says he needs me to come home," Gryffin replied with an annoyed tone. He laid his head against his headrest and let out a sigh. "I'm sorry I have to go. I promise we'll reschedule."

"It's all right. Things happen," Emery said reassuringly.

"Are you sure? I know this is so rude. You can be mad if you want to be. I totally understand."

"Gryffin, it's really okay. I'm not mad."

Gryffin studied her expression for a moment. She seemed to be sincere and understanding of the situation. "Okay. I'll drop you off at home then."

"Okay." Emery nodded.

The ride was quiet as Gryffin turned around and took Emery back home. He parked in front of her apartment building and got out of the car to open up her door. As he helped her out, he felt like he should apologize again. "I'm so sorry, Emery. I was really looking forward to spending today with you."

"We can do it another time. I'm sure whatever your brother needs you for is important."

"I'll call you," Gryffin promised.

"Sounds like a plan," Emery agreed. She walked to the front door of the building. "I'll see you around," Emery said. She flashed a quick smile and went inside.

Gryffin was alone in front of her building. *I'll see you around? Did that mean she didn't care when we see each other again? Was she telling me to not worry about seeing her anymore?* Gryffin shook off these thoughts as he recalled why he had to leave in the first place. He got back into his car and drove back to his apartment, hoping Emery wanted to see him again.

Marcus sat on the ground slumped up against the door to Gryffin's apartment, his foot tapping the ground rapidly. Was it from anxiety or something Marcus used? Gryffin didn't know. When Marcus saw his brother approaching, he stood up and met Gryffin halfway. "There you are."

"I came as soon as I could. What's going on?" Gryffin sensed something was really wrong. Marcus had an estranged look, even more so than usual, and his eyes seemed frantic.

"Not here." Marcus put his hand on Gryffin's shoulder and led him back to the apartment door. After Gryffin unlocked the door, they both went inside, and Marcus made sure the door was locked behind them. He finally said, "It's Dominic, Gryff."

"What—that dealer you give all your money to?"

"Yeah, that guy."

"What about him?"

"Something happened. I messed up, man." Marcus began pacing.

"What did you do?"

"I wanted to get some of the stuff he has, but I didn't have money for it. So I started this tab thing, where I can use as much as I want as long as I paid him back by a certain date. He let me do it because I'm a loyal customer or something like that. The day came for me to pay up, and I did. But Dom said there was interest."

"How much interest?" Gryffin's mind went to the worst scenario.

Marcus fiddled with his hands nervously. He said timidly, "Fifteen thousand."

Gryffin's stomach churned. "You owe a drug dealer fifteen

thousand dollars?" He could barely keep his composure. "What were you thinking!"

"I know, okay! I was being an idiot! But look, Gryff, I need to get him that money right away or else!"

"Or else what?"

Marcus clenched his jaw. "Or else he's going to make sure I never walk again."

Gryffin took a step backward. He rubbed his temples with his fingers as he processed what his brother had just told him. "How long do you have?"

"Until the end of the month."

Gryffin took his turn to pace.

Marcus hesitated before saying, "I know you still have money from Mom and Dad. Could you lend me some to pay Dominic back? Then I swear I'm done with him and asking you for favors."

A grave expression overcame Gryffin. Marcus had rarely ever seen this on his bother before, and when he did, it wasn't a good thing. Gryffin's voice rose as he said, "You want me to use the money Mom and Dad left me to pay off your drug dealer? You think I'll just let the hard-earned money they made get wasted on some drugs you're addicted to because you can't man up and actually take a hold of your life? What would they say, Marcus?" Gryffin's chest heaved. He closed his eyes and focused on the sliver of calmness he had left in him. "You'll just go and get high again. This won't change anything."

"I swear to you, I'll get clean, Gryffin. For real this time! I'll even get a job!" Marcus pleaded with his brother.

Gryffin stared at Marcus for a long time, not knowing whether or not to buy into this declaration. He extended his hand to his brother and proposed a deal. "I will give you the money on some terms."

"Anything," Marcus blindly agreed.

"Listen." Gryffin wasn't messing around. He looked Marcus dead in the eye. "You will pay Dominic back, and you will never see him or any dealer or drug peddler again. You will get clean and get a job. And you will move in with me until I see a change in you and I am certain you won't go back to this life."

Marcus's eyes darted from Gryffin to Gryffin's hand. He didn't want to shake it; he didn't want to take on any responsibility or give up his only form of freedom from this awful life he led. But Marcus had to pay Dominic back, or else he would come after him. Maybe he would even go after Gryffin. Marcus couldn't take that chance. He extended his hand, and just as he was about to take Gryffin's, Gryffin stated, "Don't shake it unless you swear to do all of these things, Marcus." Marcus collected his courage, gripped Gryffin's hand, and shook it. Gryffin continued to stare at him, remaining unconvinced. But Marcus did shake, and that was all Gryffin could go on right now. Gryffin went to the kitchen and opened a drawer where he took out a checkbook. He made a check out to Marcus for the amount he owed, tore it out of the book, and handed it to his brother.

"Cash this and give the money to Dominic. If I find out that you use it for anything else, you'll answer for it. Do you understand?" Gryffin stayed stoic.

"I understand," Marcus stated as he took the check from Gryffin. "Thank you, Gryff."

Gryffin turned from Marcus and walked to his room. "Go pay Dom." He shut the door.

Marcus wasn't sure if he should say anything else to his brother. He figured it would only make things worse. So he shoved the check in his pocket and left the apartment. In the next room, Gryffin sat on his bed with his head in his hands, praying that Marcus would return.

Chapter 11

Three days had passed since Gryffin had to cancel on Emery. Since then, she had not heard from him. She wondered if everything was all right. Emery even thought about calling him to make sure nothing was wrong. But she didn't want to be a nuisance if there was something going on and bother him. It had been a long time since Emery had even thought about helping someone. She hadn't cared about anyone for quite a while. She made sure she didn't, not after everything she had been through. Even so, Emery would jump at the chance to help Gryffin.

Emery sat at her kitchen table and drank a cup of coffee. She traced her finger around the rim of the mug absentmindedly. Gryffin was a popular subject on Emery's mind lately, mostly because she didn't understand him. She didn't understand why he made her think about things differently, how he could make her laugh, or why he was on her mind in general. He intrigued her; that was for certain. His outlook was unique, and the way he made the worst things seem amazing was a puzzle to her. She thought about his smile a lot too. The more she went over their time spent together, the more it became clear. Emery had feelings for Gryffin.

Was she ready for that? Was she ready to let someone back into her life after she had worked so hard to put it back together? Was she okay with relying on someone and in turn being relied upon? There was little trust Emery had to give out. But if she had to, she would give it to Gryffin. Although they had only known each other for a brief amount of time, Emery knew Gryffin would do anything for her. Would she? Yes, she would. She would for Gryffin. Emery took a sip from her mug. She puckered her lips after she had taken a swig of cold coffee. That's what she got for daydreaming about Gryffin again.

The intercom buzzed suddenly. "Miss Everett?" a male's voice said fuzzily through the small speaker. "It's Gryffin. May I come up?"

Emery was caught off guard. She quickly surveyed her apartment to see if it was in any shape for guests. There was a takeout box from The Lift on the coffee table in the living room and a blanket spread out on the couch, but other than that, it looked suitable. Emery walked over to the intercom and said, "Yes, come on up." She buzzed Gryffin in and then quickly scooped up the empty takeout box and put it in the trash can. She folded up the blanket and put it on the back of the couch. Thinking she had time before Gryffin arrived, Emery went into the bathroom and made sure she looked decent. She had just gotten home from work and was wearing a black, sleeveless, business casual dress and her leftover wavy hairstyle from the day still proved to be working for her. *This will work.*

A knock came at the door just as Emery exited the bathroom. She straightened up her dress and answered the door.

"Hey," Emery greeted Gryffin.

"Hey," Gryffin said back. "You look great."

Emery half-smiled, "I just got home and haven't changed yet." She dismissed the compliment. Emery then got a good look at Gryffin. He was wearing the same torn jeans he wore the night they met at The Lift and a long-sleeved, dark red shirt with his signature gray Converse. He always looked good to Emery, she realized. Emery caught herself gawking over him. "Come in," she recovered and let him in.

"Thanks." Gryffin walked in. He took in Emery's apartment. It was much larger than Gryffin's, painted in neutral colors and furnished in expensive furniture. It had a more modern theme than his apartment, which was dank and rustic. "Your place is really nice," Gryffin said.

"It works," Emery said as she shut the door. She watched Gryffin make his way around the kitchen and into the living room. "Did you want anything to drink?"

"No, I'm okay. Thanks."

Emery followed him into the living room. "Do you want to sit down?" She was running out of things to offer him.

"Sure." Gryffin took a seat on the end of the couch. Emery sat down too but not too close to him. She didn't know what the appropriate space was to sit from him, so she settled with sitting more toward the middle, giving them both noted space. "So ..." Emery said after several uncomfortable moments.

"So," Gryffin repeated. He clasped his hands awkwardly, twiddling his fingers. Emery waited for his explanation for what he was doing there. She knew he was out of his comfort zone. Finally, Gryffin slapped his hands down on his knees as if he'd had enough of the tension. "I'm sorry for not calling sooner. And I'm still sorry about the other day. I shouldn't have left you like that."

"I already told you, it's okay. I was just worried that something bad had happened."

"Wait." Gryffin's eyes narrowed. "You were *worried* about *me?*"

Emery realized what she had just said. "Well not worried, just ... curious."

"Curious?" Gryffin cracked a smile. "Is that what you're going with?"

There was no getting out of this, and Emery knew it. "I may have been worried. But just a little. Happy?"

Gryffin's smile was huge now, but there was something sentimental about it. Like they had hit a mark in their relationship, and he wanted to remember it. "Yes," Gryffin said.

"So is your brother okay?"

"Yes. No." Gryffin shrugged his shoulders. "I hope so."

"What do you mean?"

"Marcus hasn't always made the best decisions. Ever since our parents died, he relapsed and hasn't found a way to move on from it yet. He was in a car accident with my parents a few years ago, and he blames himself for it. Anyway, he got involved with some dealer and is taking this stuff to help him cope. I've been trying to get him back on his feet."

"I see," Emery said. She had no idea what Gryffin was going through. Emery would never have known he was being put through something so difficult and stressful because of his constant positivity toward all things. But there he sat, being open and susceptible with his own set of problems. He was human, just like Emery. For the first time, Emery understood him.

"He needed me to take care of something for him, which I'm always doing—and giving him the benefit of the doubt. But then he goes back to using and getting himself into trouble again," Gryffin vented. "I don't know what to do with him anymore. I want what's best for him—he's my brother. At the same time, if I'm always picking him up, and he knows it, what will make him really stop and get his life together?"

"You let go," Emery said. This remark caught Gryffin's attention. He wasn't expecting her to answer him. Emery had never given advice before, so this was new to her as well. "After everything I've been through, I know that you can't fix anyone. You have to let them go and fix themselves. No matter what you say or how many times you let them back in, they'll never really learn or change. Otherwise, you'll keep blaming yourself for why they are the way they are. You keep going back to try to fix them again, and they just hurt you even more."

Gryffin didn't think she was talking about his situation anymore. Although what she was saying was good advice, something else was going on inside her head. She wasn't with Gryffin anymore; she was somewhere else. Gryffin knew that if he was ever going to get beneath Emery's thick surface and dig into her past, it was now. "Is that what happened to you?"

Emery's eyes shot up at Gryffin. Her first thought was to switch the subject. No, she wouldn't this time. She would let him in. She wanted to, right? Yes, she did. Emery began her story.

"When I was thirteen, my mom passed away from cancer. My dad wasn't around, so I took care of her the best I could. But it wasn't enough. After she died, I went around to foster families. When I turned eighteen, I left the service and met a guy. I moved in with him, thinking I would start a new, better chapter in my life. Little did I know that he had a bad temper and he ..." She trailed off, recalling ghosts from her past. "He would lose it often. I told myself that he was a good guy and that I could fix him. He told me that too. So I stayed. I stayed for two years and tried with all of my might to fix that man. But the more I did, the more I realized that no amount of excuses and apologies could change him. So I finally left and made a plan. No more being pushed around. I would take care of me and only me. That's how it's been since then. That's why I haven't talked to you about it. I don't want to let you in, Gryffin. I can't."

Gryffin's heart broke for Emery. He didn't want to see her like this, eyes welling up with tears, talking about a man that mistreated her. But at the same time, she was beautiful like this. Her vulnerability toward him made him fall for her more. Gryffin sat, watching her struggle with these memories that he had brought up indirectly. Before he talked himself out of it, Gryffin scooted close to her and pulled her to him. Emery let him do so. He held her, and she cried into his shoulder. Gryffin consoled her the best he could, not asking anything more of her. When she wanted to share more with him, he would. For now, it meant the world to him that she let him in right here, right now.

"I'm sorry," Emery said in a muffled voice. She was embarrassed that she was crying in front of him, but she couldn't help it. Emery hadn't let herself cry for years.

"There is nothing to be sorry about." Gryffin held her tighter. "I'm sorry you had to go through that. You didn't deserve to be treated that way." It angered him that someone could beat up on Emery like that. How could that jerk hurt her? She was amazing and so special. Gryffin couldn't understand why anyone would want to treat someone that way. He stroked the back of her head, letting her know that he wasn't going anywhere.

Emery sniffled and sat back up, wiping the tears from her eyes. "You know, even now I still blame myself for not being able to change him. He was a good guy when he wanted to be. I feel like I gave up on him too soon. I know I shouldn't feel that way, but I do."

"Do you want to know what I think?" Gryffin asked as he wiped a single tear that rested on Emery's cheek. Emery nodded slowly. Gryffin clenched his jaw, nervousness sweeping through his body. "I think that you are amazing, and anyone who had you in their life was lucky. That guy, he was an idiot for not knowing what an incredible, smart woman he had in his life. He was the one who gave up—not you, Miss Everett."

A small smile replaced the sadness on Emery's face. A dash of red flooded her cheeks, and her heart began to become enlightened. Gryffin took her hands in his. "I want you to know that I think you are crazy beautiful inside and out. You're strong, and you may try to act like you don't care about anything, but I know you do. You've been through so much in such a small amount of time that you've had to grow up quickly, and that's caused you to be wiser than your years." A food of relief washed over Gryffin's heart and mind. He was finally letting all of these things he was feeling out. He continued, "Even though our whole reason for hanging out was for you to see this world in a different perspective, I wouldn't change a thing about you." He spoke with confidence and sincerity. "You're perfect to me, Emery."

Emery felt her insides melting. Her head was spinning, and her heartbeat was like a drum pounding in her ears. How could she respond to this? Emery wasn't good at taking compliments, mostly because she had never received so many and so abruptly. So she fell back on her signature sarcasm to win over Gryffin. "I thought it was Miss Everett." She playfully smiled.

Gryffin smirked and gave her hands a gentle squeeze. "You're perfect, *Miss Everett*."

Emery felt the heat rush to her cheeks again. At the same time, she felt tears forming in her eyes. A weight she had been bearing for three years was suddenly gone. No one had ever been so honest and endearing to her before. Gryffin was someone she wanted to start over with. She had no idea how to tell him that. There he was, looking at her with those deep brown eyes that pulled her in swiftly and smoothly. Emery was unable to find the words to say to Gryffin, so she wrapped her arms around him and hugged him again.

Gryffin rested his head on hers and closed his eyes. Nothing in the world ever felt better than this did. He wanted to do this forever. Emery didn't want it to end either. Gryffin and Emery leaned against the couch and continued to hold each other tightly, as if they were holding all of their deepest secrets together for only them to know.

Chapter 12

*E*mery wore a smile a mile wide after her and Gryffin's heart-to-heart. Gryffin went home that day feeling like a million dollars, a feeling music didn't even give him. The two didn't know where to go after that, but they wanted to go together. They met for lunch the next day and went to the movies that night. The day after, it was a walk in the park and another boat ride. They hadn't completed another task from the list for a few days. Gryffin decided it was time to cross another task off. He called Emery and told her to meet him on the outskirts of town, where there was only forest for miles around them. Emery agreed and met Gryffin there that afternoon, not knowing what the day held for her.

"Did you bring what I asked?" Gryffin asked as Emery got out of her car. He was wearing a pair of gym shorts, tennis shoes, and a cutoff, ready to take a trek into the wilderness.

"Yep, a water bottle and a towel." Emery held up the items.

Gryffin held out his hand, waiting for Emery to give them to him. When she did, he put them in his backpack, zipped it back up, and slung it over his shoulders. "And you're wearing clothes you don't mind getting dirty, right?" he asked.

"I am." Emery nodded.

"Okay, let's get going then." Gryffin motioned for her to follow him. Gryffin and Emery walked into the wooded area next to the road. They walked through the forest for a good twenty minutes. It was shaded and wet from the condensation of the morning dew. Small sunbeams shot through the gaps between the trees above. Gryffin and Emery didn't talk very much on the walk to their destination. Emery was okay with this; she enjoyed the tranquility of nature as she hiked into it. Gryffin wanted this task to remain a mystery, so he stayed quiet, occasionally making sure Emery was okay behind him.

In a small clearing ahead of them, Emery could make out a large cliff with a waterfall pouring over it and into a pool below. Next to this pond of water was a hut made out of wood and leaves. Gryffin stopped when they reached it and turned to Emery, beaming.

"Welcome to my getaway." Gryffin extended his arms as to show the entirety of the place to her. "Pretty great, right?"

"Its beautiful here." Emery took in their surroundings.

Gryffin walked over to the small hut. It was about the size of a woodshed, made out of logs and sticks. There was no door to the hut, just a rectangular opening. Gryffin let Emery go in before him, following her inside. There were two small chairs and a lantern inside. Gryffin set down his backpack and took out the Emery's water bottle and handed to her. Emery thanked him and took a drink of cool, refreshing water. Gryffin fished out his own water and did the same. The hike to Gryffin's hideaway wasn't strenuous, but it was a warm walk with uneven terrain. It was more walking in the wilderness than Emery had ever done.

Gryffin poured some water over his head to wet his hair and the back of his neck. "What do you think?"

"This is nice, Gryffin. How did you find this place?"

"My brother and I built it with my dad when we were kids. We would come out here during the summer and spend days here." Gryffin took a seat in one of the chairs.

"How long did it take you to build it?"

"Not long, a few days." Gryffin took another drink of water. "It may look old and decrepit, but it's survived all sorts of wear and tear out here."

"So, what's the meaning behind this whole adventure?" Emery crossed her arms.

Gryffin leaned forward, putting his elbows on his knees. He examined Emery before beginning. "Memories can either haunt us or enlighten us. We both have been through things that have broken us. So it's important to hold onto the good things that have happened to us in the past. If we let everything go, we aren't us anymore. We become a shell."

Emery shifted her weight uncomfortably. She was still getting used to this whole honesty thing. She looked away from Gryffin and said, "What if all the memories we have are bad ones?"

"You have no good memories?" Gryffin found that hard to believe.

"No." Emery swallowed.

Gryffin thought for a moment. "What about your mother?

Don't you remember anything good before she …" He didn't know if he should finish.

Emery put her hands on the back of the chair and leaned forward. "Everything good about my mother is gone, Gryffin. All I remember is her being in that hospital bed and the doctors saying there was nothing more they could do."

Gryffin didn't respond. He knew Emery was hurting. Emery recognized that she was becoming angry. Talking about her mother hit a nerve in Emery. She straightened back up. "I'm sorry, but any good memories of my mom died with her."

"Do you blame yourself?" Gryffin asked.

"Of course I blame myself, Gryffin. I was her daughter. I should have been able to do more for her."

"But there was nothing you could do. She was sick," Gryffin reasoned with her.

Emery wouldn't let herself lose her composure again. "I still should have saved her somehow. It wasn't fair. Why did she have to go and not me?"

Gryffin carefully thought out his answer. He stood and went to her. Speaking earnestly, he said, "Because you were meant to do something else here."

Emery didn't believe that. She shook her head and scoffed, "Like what? Get involved with an abusive boyfriend and become a callused, miserable person?"

"No. Maybe it was to find me."

Emery met Gryffin's eyes. Was that the reason she was still here? Could it be that it was to be with Gryffin? All of this was so much to handle, yet she could because Gryffin was there handling it with her.

Gryffin's said, "You have no idea what you've done to me since you walked into my life, Miss Everett."

"What do you mean?"

"I mean," Gryffin took her hands again, "I have never been happier in my entire life than I am right now."

Emery was drawn into his eyes again.

"In your own strange, realist way," Gryffin said, "you made me look at things differently too."

Emery stayed silent as Gryffin opened up to her. He did feel something for her after all. Her heart was beating rapidly again. How did he have this effect on her? She didn't care; she didn't want it to stop.

"If you don't have any good memories from your past, then let's make some. Right here, right now." Gryffin went to his backpack and took out a small disposable camera.

"What are you doing?" Emery asked him.

"Documenting the start of a new set of memories." He stood next to her and put the camera out so the lens was facing them. "Together," Gryffin added. Before Emery could comment on this, Gryffin smiled widely for the camera. "Say cheese!" He snapped the camera as Emery was giggling.

"That was probably horrible!" Emery figured the camera caught a weird expression on her face because of her laughing.

"No, it was great!" Gryffin protested.

Emery took the camera. "How do you know? We can't even look at the picture!" She was still laughing. "Why do you even have this? It's such an old-style camera."

"Hey! It's *vintage*!" Gryffin was laughing now too. "If you think it was a bad picture, we'll just have to take another one." He grabbed the camera from Emery and stretched out his arm again. "Smile this time, okay?"

"Fine," Emery said. She smiled widely. He snapped another picture and wound the film reel with his thumb. "We're going to use this entire camera up today, just so you know!" Gryffin shouted as he ran out of the hut.

"What? No! Gryffin, I hate pictures! That was a onetime thing!" She ran out behind him.

The rest of the day, Gryffin and Emery spent every moment together. They went exploring deeper into the woods, Gryffin snapping photos of Emery the whole time. When they came back to Gryffin's hideaway, they took off their shoes and socks and jumped into the pond. To Emery's surprise, Gryffin climbed to the top of the tall cliff above the waterfall and jumped off it. Gryffin coaxed her to do the same, and, with hesitation, Emery agreed. She wanted to impress him. But after climbing halfway up the giant rock, her fearlessness quickly receded.

"Can I just jump off here?" Emery yelled down to Gryffin, who was about twelve feet below her.

"You're supposed to jump off the very top!" Gryffin shouted back.

Emery looked down; everything seemed so small. "This is close enough."

"You're almost to the top!" Gryffin encouraged her. "Come on, just a few more feet. You can do it!" He clicked the shutter button on the camera.

"I'm calling it!" Emery yelled. She pushed off the ledge with her hands and feet and went plummeting into the water.

When she came up to the surface, she saw Gryffin shaking his head from the shore. "So close."

Emery splashed him, making Gryffin put down the camera and do a full-on cannonball into the water. They played like this for hours. Emery felt like a kid again. She felt a new breath of life in her lungs, one that had been taken from her long ago.

That night, Gryffin made a campfire. He had also brought marshmallows and other necessities for s'mores. They found two long sticks and stuck the tips into the fire to make them more susceptible to roasting marshmallows. As they did this, Emery asked, "Why haven't you played me a song?"

Gryffin smiled. "You want me to play you a song?"

"Well, yeah. You're in a band, you know. So I figured at some point I would hear you play or sing or something."

"You heard me play at The Lift the night we met."

"Yeah, but I didn't really know you then. I do now."

Gryffin was catching on. "So what you're saying is that you want me to invite you to a show."

Emery felt a touch of shyness come over her, "Yeah, I want to support you. You're doing this whole list for me, so I want to do something for you."

"Okay." Gryffin thought it was sweet that she wanted to be there for him. "Miss Everett, would you like to come to my next show?"

Emery laughed at the formal invitation. "Why yes, Mr. Brooks, I would love to attend."

Gryffin smirked. They sat together for the remainder of the evening, talking and eating s'mores around the campfire. Nervousness skulked in Gryffin's mind. The reality set in that Emery would be at his next show—the show where he would play the song he wrote about her.

Chapter 13

That night, Gryffin came home around ten o'clock. He dropped his backpack on the floor after coming in the front door. Marcus was sitting on the couch in the living room watching TV.

"Hey, where were you all day?" Marcus asked.

"Out," Gryffin said blandly.

"What—you aren't going to tell me?"

"I was with a friend."

"Why are you being like this?" Marcus was getting irritated that Gryffin was giving him the cold shoulder. He had been staying with Gryffin for about a week now, and Gryffin barely said a few words to him.

"I'm tired, Marcus. I want to go to sleep," Gryffin said from his bedroom doorway.

"Is this because of the money? I told you I would pay you back."

Gryffin chortled. "Yeah, how are you going to do that when you don't have a job?" He began to close his bedroom door.

"I do now," Marcus chimed.

Gryffin swung his door open. "What?"

"I got a job today!" Marcus exclaimed.

"You're not kidding me, are you?" Gryffin didn't want to get his hopes up.

"I swear, Gryff. I start Monday."

Gryffin crossed his arms. "Where are you working?"

"The gas station down the street. It's only part-time, but it'll work for now, right?"

"Yeah." Gryffin nodded, his cold mood melting. "It'll work."

Marcus felt relief come over him; he had taken a step in the right direction.

Gryffin scratched his head and took a seat in the chair next to the couch. "So how are you feeling today?"

"Like my head is going to explode," Marcus said. He had not been using for a little over a week now; at least that's what he was telling Gryffin. Gryffin did see a slight change in him though. He wasn't so pale anymore, and he didn't sleep all the time like he used to. Marcus also appeared to be more put together; he wasn't so on edge or as apprehensive as he was when he was using.

Gryffin kicked up the chair's leg rest and stretched out his legs. He lay back on the chair and put his hands behind his head. Before he drifted off to sleep, Marcus heard him say, "I'm proud of you." With that, Gryffin fell asleep. Marcus felt like he had accomplished something great that day. He too, went to sleep relieved and relaxed.

The night of the concert came, and Gryffin was a nervous wreck. This was so strange; he had never felt this way before. Music was his forte, where he drew confidence from. Tonight was completely different though. He played through the songs backstage over and over on his guitar and warmed up as early as he could. Escalates was to play at nine o'clock at a medium-sized theater designed to hold a couple hundred people. Gryffin got a look at the crowd before they went on. The place was packed; they had sold out the show. While Derek, Alec, and Paige were thrilled, Gryffin showed no interest in the fact that the entire theatre was filled up with their fans. He was thinking about only one fan—Emery.

A few hours before Escalates had left for the venue, Gryffin called Emery and asked if she wanted to ride with him. She said she didn't want to get in the way and would come separately. Gryffin also asked if she wanted to stand backstage and watch them. To that, Emery also said no; she wanted to be in the crowd and get the full effect of the concert experience like everyone else. Mainly, Emery did not want to be a bother. She had never met the band-mates before and didn't want to be that annoying roadie that always hung around. Wait, was she a roadie now? Emery laughed at the thought. No, she wasn't cut out for that kind of life.

Emery arrived a few minutes before the band went on. She stood near the back to avoid the densest parts of the crowd. There were some real fans at this show, sporting shirts with the band logo on it, and some even started chanting their name right before the show was about to start. Emery watched as the lights in the room dimmed, making the crowd cheer and go wild. She could vaguely make out the band walk onto the stage and take their places in the darkness. The spotlights flooded the stage with multicolored lighting, illuminating the band members for all to see. The crowed clapped and yelled for Escalates. Emery clapped too and even gave a whoop for them.

Something felt wrong. Emery watched as the bassist and lead guitarist waited for Gryffin to give the signal to start. Gryffin stood like a statue, frozen with fear. Emery didn't recognize this expression on Gryffin; he was fearless to her. He jammed his hand into his pocket and retrieved a pick, then went back to standing still. Emery wondered what was going on with him. Why was he acting this way? The bassist, Alec, patted Gryffin on the shoulder and mouthed something that Emery couldn't make out. Gryffin nodded to him. Then he snapped out of whatever daze he was in and gave a small nod to the girl percussionist behind him. With that, they began to play their first song.

The song was upbeat and made everyone want to jump up and down. Emery tapped her foot along to the beat. Gryffin then sang the first line of their opening song. Emery's heart melted. His voice was powerful and magical. She couldn't take her eyes off him. He played his heart out, getting the crowd to clap along, messing around with his bandmates, having a great time. The audience loved him. The energy Gryffin put out, they gave him right back. During one of the songs, Gryffin stepped away from the microphone and let the audience sing for him. She was shocked that at least three-fourths of the crowd knew the words and sang them right back to him. Why hadn't Emery heard of these guys before?

Even if she had never met Gryffin at The Lift that night, she still would have loved this band.

At the halfway point of Escalates' set, Gryffin told everyone that they would be performing a new song. The crowd cheered at this, excited to see what the band had up their sleeve. Gryffin then said something surprising. "This song is about someone I met. She's here tonight, actually." Emery heard some people let out "Aww." She blushed. Gryffin continued, "She means a lot to me, and I want her to know that. This song is for her."

A man yelled, "Atta boy!" Emery laughed; this was so surreal. Gryffin had actually written a song for her. She waited with bated breath for it to begin.

The beginning of the song was calm and easy, and as it went on, it built up to be powerful and moving. The lyrics went like this:

> I believe it was a Friday night
> When you walked right into my life,
> And I couldn't move or speak.
> I wondered right then if you could see
> What I was thinking.
>
> My heart didn't want to wonder anymore.
> My spirits began to soar.
> Everything I ever feared mattered no more
> Because, darling, you're all this heart could hope for.
>
> I believe it was half past nine
> When I caught that wondrous sight
> Of you smiling back at me.
> I wondered right then if you could see
> What I was thinking—oh, I was thinking.

My heart didn't want to wonder anymore.
My spirits began to soar.
Everything I ever feared mattered no more
Because, darling, you're all this heart could hope for.

I know you find it hard to believe,
But you're the best thing that ever happened to me.
I know you don't think it's true.
But, darling, I think I am falling for you.

My heart didn't want to wonder anymore.
My spirits began to soar.
Everything I ever feared mattered no more
Because, darling, you're all this heart could hope for.

Emery was speechless. This was such a magnificent gesture, and it was all for her. Gryffin thanked the crowd when the song came to an end. His bandmates were all pleased with their performances. The entire crowd erupted with applause. They loved the song too. Gryffin smiled broadly and surveyed the audience, looking for Emery. He couldn't see her, but he knew she was out there somewhere, watching him. He took a deep breath and went back to the show.

The rest of the show flew by. They played three more songs before the final song, which was the one everyone seemed to like the most. When Escalates was done with their set, they took a bow and thanked everyone for coming out. Gryffin immediately jumped off the stage and went to look for Emery. People gathered around him, shaking his hand and giving him slaps on the back, making it hard for Gryffin to spot her.

Emery saw him coming and thought about waiting in the back at first. But this man had written a song for her and performed it in front of all of these people. The least she could do was meet him halfway.

In the middle of the crowd, Emery and Gryffin caught sight of each other. Gryffin quickened his pace and moved through the adoring fans to get to her. Emery tried to be more polite as she passed people, saying excuse me and apologizing when someone bumped into her. The last person she ran into was Gryffin. Emery said, "So who's this girl you wrote about?"

For a moment, Gryffin bought into her sarcasm. Then he realized she was joking, but he couldn't play along. This was the defining moment for them. He had to make it clear. "You, Miss Everett," he said with a heartfelt grin.

The absence of sarcasm threw Emery off. For some reason, she couldn't catch her breath. It was stuck in her throat as Gryffin came closer to her. "I don't know what we are, but I do know this: I want to be with you, Miss Everett." He put out his hand. "Will you let me?"

This was all a surprise to Emery. She had no idea he felt so strongly about her. She wanted to be with him, but she was afraid. The more comfortable people get, the more their true colors show. What if Gryffin wasn't what she thought him to be? What if under all of that chivalry and kindness was anger and unresolved conflict building up? It had happened to her before, and it could happen again. Emery knew what she had to say. She took his hand.

"I will." Emery smiled back at him. This felt right.

Gryffin's heart leapt from his chest, and his soul flew. He pulled her in and held her tightly. The people around them cheered and whooped for them, seeing young love blossom. Gryffin gently kissed the top of Emery's forehead and smiled down at her. This is what he had been waiting for. Emery knew that no matter what came next, Gryffin would make it all right somehow. She could do this, she thought; she could get through this life thing.

Chapter 14

"**Y**ou're the infamous Emery Everett," Derek said as he shook Emery's hand. "I was wondering when you would make an appearance."

Escalates sat backstage, unwinding after the show they had just performed. It was a little area, painted in royal red and furnished with records hanging from the wall. Derek and Paige sat on a black pleather couch, and Alec was laying out on the ground next to them. When Gryffin said he wanted to introduce Emery to his bandmates, she was nervous. His friends were crazy talented, and Emery was just … Emery. Gryffin reassured her that they would love her and just to be herself. So, with hesitancy, Emery agreed to meet them.

"This is Derek, Paige, and Alec." Gryffin pointed to each of his friends.

"Nice to meet you all," she greeted.

"Wow, nice job, Gryff." Alec was stricken with how gorgeous Emery was.

"Hey, watch it, buddy," Gryffin jested. He put his arm around Emery as if he was protecting her from Alec's remarks.

Paige instantly noticed this. "Hold up." She put her hands out in a stop motion. "Are you two together?"

Gryffin gave them a smug smile, confirming her theory.

"Finally!" Derek let out an exasperated breath. "It's about time!"

"Shut up." Gryffin's face turned a light red in embarrassment.

"What a way to do it though. Props, bro." Alec saluted Gryffin.

They all agreed. Emery saw how much Gryffin's friends cared about him. The way they talked to him, the way they gave each other a hard time. It was kind of like the relationship she and Gryffin had, only on a family basis.

"How did you like the show?" Paige asked Emery.

"You all were amazing," Emery said. "I had no idea your fan base was so big."

Derek and Gryffin exchanged looks. "Neither did we. We sold out the show tonight."

"That was probably one of the best performances we put on," Gryffin said. "It was crazy how into the music the audience was."

"It was awesome," Derek agreed.

"It was tiring." Alec spoke from the floor.

Paige kicked his leg. "You're always tired."

"I'm a big man. I need more food if I'm going to play a show like that," Alec countered.

Derek patted his stomach. "Speaking of which, did you guys want to grab a slice or something?"

Alec shot up in excitement. "Let's go." He was already walking toward the exit. "Nice meeting you, Emery," he said kindly as he passed her.

Paige and Derek got up to follow him out. "You guys coming?"

Gryffin looked to Emery for her thoughts. Emery nodded. "Yeah, I'll go."

"I guess we're all going then." Gryffin was happy Emery wanted to hang out with his friends. They followed Derek and Paige out of the theatre.

They ate at a local pizza joint not far from the theater. Derek, Alec, and Gryffin ate two entire pizzas by themselves. Paige and Emery decided it would be best to share one since their stomachs couldn't handle quite as much capacity as the boys could. The two girls ordered a pepperoni pizza and ate a little over half of it. When everyone was done devouring the food, the conversation began.

"How did you guys get together?" Emery was curious about Escalates' beginnings.

Derek first spoke. "Well, Alec and I knew each other from high school, so we always played together for fun. Then we decided we wanted to try to get a little more serious, so we held auditions for a drummer. Obviously, that's how we met Paige."

"And they're lucky they did," Paige poked.

"Hey, it was between you and that one guy who only knew how to play triangle," Alec poked back.

"Okay, fine." Paige waved the comment off.

"Anyway, what's really interesting is how we met this guy."

Derek pointed to Gryffin. "I would go running in that park down-town every day."

"Which he has obviously stopped doing." Alec laughed.

Derek brushed the joke off. "I would always see this guy sitting on this bench by the pond playing his guitar. And I thought he was good, like really good. He was always playing two songs, and they sounded like originals. One day I decided to take my guitar with me and ask him if I could join in. Well, he wasn't there that day. So I go home and think, *I'll try again tomorrow.* Then, just as I'm about to go inside my house, I hear that same song this guy has been playing in the park for months. I walk around to the back of my house, and wouldn't you know it—Gryffin is playing in the backyard of the house next-door."

"We had been neighbors for years and never knew it," Gryffin said.

"That was when you lived with your parents," Derek observed.

"Yeah, a long time ago," Gryffin said absently.

Derek picked the story back up. "I asked him if he wanted to jam with us, he said yes, and here we are."

"Talk about small world," Emery said, impressed with the story.

"I know—right? Crazy," Derek agreed.

"We've been a family since," Gryffin concluded.

"And now you're a part of it, Emery." Paige nudged Emery.

Emery chuckled. "I'm not cut out to be a roadie."

"I just mean you're an honorary member. Any of Gryffin's friends are included at all times," Paige explained. "Besides, it will be nice to have another girl to talk to when you can make it to shows." She smiled.

"What's wrong with having all brothers?" Alec shot at her.

"Nothing, except when you can be boneheads," she shot back at him. She turned to Emery. "Trust me, the testosterone gets to you."

Emery laughed. She and Paige talked the rest of the time. Surprisingly, Paige was a sweet, lighthearted girl, which Emery would not have guessed because of her rough rocker exterior. She loved kids, volunteered at an elderly center, and worked at an animal shelter. Emery could see her and Paige getting along just fine. As for the other two guys, they joked with Emery like they had known her for ages. Emery enjoyed that about them; she immediately felt included. Emery had found her first real set of friends there in that pizzeria.

Gryffin enjoyed watching Emery talk and laugh with Paige. When Derek and Alec gave her a hard time, she sassed them right back. Gryffin kept thinking how happy he was that she was with him. When Gryffin caught Emery's eye for a moment, he winked at her, and she rolled her eyes and went back to conversing with Paige. This was how he had always wanted things to be—with his best friends and with the girl he loved. The only thing that could make it better was Marcus's full recovery. He hoped one day Emery would meet him, but right now, he didn't want her to. Not until Marcus went back into society soberly and with integrity.

One week of being together turned into a month, and a month turned into two. Gryffin and Emery were never happier. They spent all their free time together. Emery went to Gryffin's band practices when she was able, and Gryffin took her out after she got out of work. They were falling more and more for each other. Gryffin had Emery over for dinner at his apartment when he knew Marcus wouldn't be home. He still avoided the subject of the two of them meeting, which confused Emery. She didn't understand why he was always making excuses for them not to meet. She didn't press the subject; Gryffin wasn't going to change his mind. Their lives were peaking, Emery thought, and she didn't want to do anything to compromise that.

"I have a question," Emery said after they had just finished a gourmet dinner of spaghetti at Gryffin's apartment.

Gryffin wiped his mouth with his napkin. "Yes, Miss Everett."

She still got chills when he said that. Quickly, she composed herself. "How can you afford this place and not be working?"

Gryffin raised his eyebrows like he was surprised she had the nerve to ask. Emery didn't really care. Gryffin cleared his throat. "Well, when my parents died, Marcus and I split the money they left us. My mom was a nurse, and my dad was a lawyer. So they had quite a bit of money. I used it to move here, and I have enough to last me a long time until I want to get a bigger place or house."

"What about Marcus? What did he use his money for?"

Gryffin knew the question was innocent, but he didn't want to talk about Marcus. "He just spent it unwisely."

"Oh, right. You said he got involved with some bad people." Emery took a fork full of spaghetti and put it in her mouth.

"Yeah," Gryffin said, "we just dealt with it differently."

"How did you?" Emery cocked her head to the side.

"Me?" Gryffin had never been asked that before. He thought for a moment. "I guess I just decided that being upset and hating the world for what happened to them wasn't going to bring them back. I looked to the better things we still had. Marcus didn't."

"You're one of a kind, Gryffin Brooks." Emery slid her hand across the table and took Gryffin's. "You know that, right?"

It was his turn to feel his stomach warm up and his muscles tense up. He bowed his head down to her hand and kissed it softly. "How did I get so lucky?"

Emery grinned. "I don't know. How did you?" Her snarky attitude was back.

Gryffin got up from his seat. "Oh really?" He pulled out her chair and picked her up out of her seat.

Emery erupted in laughter. "Yes, really!"

Gryffin spun around with her in his arms and then set her down. After their laughter had settled, Gryffin tucked a piece of loose hair behind her ear. "I don't think I'll ever know."

What Gryffin didn't know was that to Emery, he was her miracle. Not the other way around. Before Gryffin, she had been a mess. She had been a lifeless, soulless, body who couldn't care less about anyone or anything. Now she was happy. Truly, deeply happy. And all she wanted was to make him feel the same way.

The front door opened, and in walked Marcus. He was wearing his gas station uniform—a bright blue polo and tan khakis. Marcus didn't realize that Gryffin and Emery were there at first. It wasn't until he shut the door and locked it that he noticed them standing in the kitchen.

"Man! You scared me!" Marcus exclaimed at the sight of a surprised Gryffin and Emery.

"Marcus, I thought you were working late tonight." Gryffin couldn't believe Marcus had just ruined a moment.

"They let me off early. I texted you." Marcus held up his cell phone. He smiled at Emery. "Hi, you must be Gryffin's friend. I'm Marcus." He walked over to her and shook her hand.

"Nice to meet you," Emery said, finally putting a face to a name. He was not at all like Gryffin had described. Marcus had short, closely cropped hair and was cleanly shaven. He had kind eyes and a nice smile compared to the shaggy, not-put-together image Gryffin had given her.

"You too. I've heard great things about you," Marcus kindly added.

"Really?" Emery turned to Gryffin. He never talked about his brother, so it was a shock that he talked to Marcus about her. "Interesting."

"Well, don't let me interrupt. I'm going to head to bed." Marcus began to walk to the bathroom.

"Are you staying here?" Emery asked Marcus.

"Yeah, I have been for a couple months now. Didn't Gryffin tell you?" Marcus replied.

"No." Emery shot a look to Gryffin, who wouldn't meet her eyes. "He didn't."

"Oh." Marcus sensed the uncomfortable tension and decided it was time to check out. "Well I'm going to grab a shower and then just hang in your room until you guys are done, Gryff. Have a good night, Miss."

"Emery," she corrected him. "You can call me Emery."

Marcus nodded. "Good night, Emery." He disappeared into the bathroom, closing the door behind him.

Gryffin instantaneously felt the tension. Emery crossed her arms, not a good sign. "So your brother is staying with you? As in the brother you rarely talk to?"

"Yeah, he is," Gryffin admitted.

"Why didn't you tell me? Wait, have you been letting me come here when he isn't over?" Gryffin didn't speak. "You're embarrassed of him, aren't you?"

Gryffin stared at the wall in front of him.

"Gryffin, tell me what's going on." Emery awaited a response patiently.

"You don't understand," Gryffin said. "He's still in the process of getting off whatever drug he was using. He may look put together, but I promise he isn't."

"What are you talking about? He apparently has a job, and he doesn't even look like a drug addict. You made him seem like this awful human being who's just so messed up."

"He is!" Gryffin's voice raised a little but not enough to be yelling. "You never saw what he was like when I had to pick him up after a night on the town! Babbling, completely dirty, unpredictable—one time he didn't even remember his name! He's never stayed clean before; he's always gone back to using."

Emery didn't like this side of Gryffin. She understood why he was upset, but he didn't need to talk to her in that tone. "How long has it been since he used, Gryffin?" Emery calmly asked.

Gryffin ran his hands through his hair and then rested them on his hips. "Almost two months."

"Do you think that maybe you're just scared that he'll let you down again?" Emery rationalized. "Is that why you don't want me to meet him, because you're afraid he'll relapse and I'll see it?"

Gryffin didn't look at her; he was ashamed of his behavior. He was ashamed that he was hiding his brother from her. Emery took a step closer to him so she could talk quieter. "I get it, okay?

Remember, I was with an alcoholic for two years. I was really good at coming up with excuses as to why people shouldn't meet him. I understand, Gryffin. It's okay to be afraid."

He looked at her somberly. "I just want my brother back."

"I know you do," Emery said as she pulled him in for a hug. "I know."

From the other side of the bathroom door, Marcus stood with his head against the door. He had heard the entire the conversation, and the cruel reality of what he had become and who he had hurt set in. More than ever, he wanted to prove to his brother that he would make it on his own. No matter the cost.

Chapter 15

*G*ryffin wanted to cross another item off his list of perspective-changing things for him and Emery to do. After being together for five months now, they had strayed from their challenge. Gryffin picked up Emery on a sunny Sunday afternoon and drove her out to the countryside. Emery didn't see a picnic blanket or basket, so that wasn't on the list. She didn't care where they were going or what they were doing. She was with him, and that was all she cared about.

The car came to a stop as Gryffin pulled off the road and parked in the grass. "This will work," Gryffin said as he exited the vehicle. He helped Emery out, taking her hand as she got out of the car. He closed the door behind her, and they walked hand in hand into a large field of wheat. Emery was wearing a skirt today because it was warmer outside, causing her legs to itch as they passed through the waist-high barley field. They walked for a few minutes until Gryffin was satisfied with a spot in the middle.

She knew him. Yet she didn't know him. There was so much mystery behind those dark eyes of his. She wished she could look through them, just once, to see what he saw. He had a spark that Emery had never seen in anyone else. A spark that one might see in children when they opened their Christmas presents or when they saw fireworks for the first time. The thing that made him full of awe and wonderment. That's what Emery wanted. She wanted to feel and be everything he was. Life radiated from him and onto others, making them stop what they were doing to just smile for a moment at how amazing this place we call Earth is and how precious every breath is too.

"May I show you something, Emery?" He looked at her with keen eyes, extending his hand. She nodded slowly, uncertainty rushing over her. Gryffin rarely called Emery by her first name. She took his hand, and he smiled at her, the same grin he always gave when he was excited about something. Gryffin turned to fully face her. He placed his other hand on top of the one that was holding his. "Close your eyes," Gryffin instructed. Emery gave him an odd look at first, but then she did as he said. She closed her eyes and didn't hear anything for a few moments. Emery became anxious, wondering what surprise he had in store.

Gryffin said, "Do hear that?"

Emery didn't hear anything out of the ordinary. "No …"

"Listen." Gryffin gave her hand a small squeeze. "You'll hear it."

She tried to focus but only heard the small breeze blowing through the wheat and grass. "What am I supposed to be listening for?" She felt impatience coming on. Gryffin didn't answer her. Emery opened her eyes to see what he was doing. Gryffin had his eyes shut. He seemed to be at peace, even more so than he usually did. Emery watched him for a moment, studying him. Gryffin opened his eyes after a moment, as if he could feel her stare resting on him. He turned his head to the left and then to the right, examining his surroundings.

Gryffin directed his eyes back to Emery. "What do you hear, Emery?" he asked inquisitively yet knowingly.

"I hear the wind. I hear the grass and the wheat rustling," Emery said, like she was hoping that was the right answer.

"Do you?" he asked in way that made Emery question herself.

She nodded, not understanding what he was getting at.

Gryffin closed his eyes again. "I hear music. Music playing vibrantly all around us." He turned his head to the left, eyes still shut. "Over there are the strings." He turned his head to the left. "Over there are the winds." Gryffin opened his eyes again. "Behind you, percussion."

Emery gave Gryffin a curious look. He took a step closer to her. "Don't you hear it, Emery? Do you hear the melody sweeping through the field? I do." Gryffin breathed in the fresh air. "I hear it all." He focused his attention back on her.

She didn't know what to say. Emery didn't hear anything that he was claiming to hear. So she closed her eyes again and played along. But something strange happened.

She heard the music.

Emery opened her eyes quickly, looking around her. She saw no one else around them, and no car or building was in sight. Emery couldn't help but laugh. Gryffin laughed too. She turned around and watched the wind make patterns in the field of wheat around them. With each gust, the melody struck the most beautiful sound she had ever heard. The song was a moderate tempo, relaxing yet powerful. From behind Emery, Gryffin reached around her and took her hands. He then lifted them up over her head and began waving them back and forth, as if she was conducting the sound the wind was making. Emery laughed even more, glee filling her spirit—the same glee Gryffin showed every day.

Gryffin continued to do this for a few more seconds. He then eased off so Emery was the only maestro of the orchestra. She allowed the wind to guide her gestures, moving her arms up and down. She knew it was all in her head, but still, the imaginary orchestra filled her with such emotion. Emery felt something wet in her eyes. Tears? Was she tearing up? No, why would this have any emotional effect on her? It didn't make sense. Emery slowly brought her hands back down to her sides. The wheat brushed up against her fingers as the wind blew them around. The music was gone now.

Gryffin walked in front of her and saw that she was crying. Emery was not embarrassed anymore. Not since the first time he had seen her cry did she worry about keeping her emotions in check. He looked at her with a meaningful gaze and said, "Let me take this one." Emery sniffled and nodded. She knew why she was crying now.

Emery watched as Gryffin turned from her and back to the field before them. He raised his hands and began conducting another melody. He seemed so lost in the music, like everything he had was being poured into it. He twirled his hand up in the air as if he wanted his orchestra to repeat the song. Gryffin walked back to Emery. He extended his hand to her. Emery took it without hesitation. Gryffin took her to him, and they began to dance slowly to the melody he had just conducted.

"You don't have to do this alone anymore, Emery," Gryffin whispered. "You're free."

Emery couldn't do anything but smile and let more tears loose. She knew the tears were because she had someone to cry on now. Emery had always thought she would end up alone and neglected after being with someone so abusive. Emery had been told all of her life that she wasn't enough, and she had believed it. Now, she was. She was enough for him, and Gryffin would never ask anything more of her. Emery rested her head on Gryffin's shoulder, and he guided the rest of their dance. Neither of them said anything. They just moved to the music that the wind created. The music that had been there all along.

"Is it working, Miss Everett?" Gryffin asked after they had gotten back into the car. "Is my list making you see things a little differently?"

Emery didn't know how else to tell him, so she leaned over and kissed him. Gryffin hadn't expected that, and his face said it all. When Emery pulled back and saw the astonishment and glee that was evident on him, she chuckled.

"I'll take that as a yes," Gryffin cheered. "Wait." He reached over to the glove compartment and took out a disposable camera. Emery was accustomed to this by now. They had gone through three of them already. "Can we do that again?"

"No!" Emery exclaimed. "We are not going to be *that couple* that takes pictures of themselves kissing!"

Gryffin pleaded with his eyes. "Just on the cheek?"

Emery wasn't buying it.

"For the sake of keeping memories?" Gryffin played the sentiment card.

He had her on that one. "Okay but just on the cheek." She made sure he understood.

Emery scooted closer to him and planted a small kiss on his cheek. He gave the camera an overly cheesy smile and captured the photo. This would be Gryffin's favorite photo of them for all time.

Chapter 16

*g*ryffin came home to Marcus frantically pacing around the living room.

"What's got you so worked up?" Gryffin asked as he tossed his keys on the counter.

"Nothing, I'm fine." Marcus walked passed Gryffin and headed toward the door.

"Hey—wait, man." Gryffin grabbed his arm, stopping him. "What's going on?"

"Let me go," Marcus said gravely.

"Not until you tell me what happened."

"I don't want you involved, okay?" Marcus moved his arm so Gryffin's hand slid off of him. "I'll figure it out."

"Marcus, I'm your brother. Let me help you." Gryffin tried a calmer approach.

Marcus stopped in the doorway for a moment. He wanted to tell Gryffin that the gas station had fired him. He wanted to tell him he had gotten a new job. But then he would have to reveal what that job was, and Gryffin wouldn't stand for it. "I can do this myself," Marcus stated and shut the door behind him.

Gryffin waited up for Marcus that night. When Marcus didn't come home, Gryffin called him. There was no answer. Gryffin called Emery and told her about Marcus's strange behavior. She suggested that maybe things were just tough at work and he needed some space. Something felt off about it though. Marcus had been clean for five months now. Was he using again? Gryffin would not allow his mind to go to that place. Instead, he picked up his guitar and decided to write a song. There was another gig coming up, and he wanted to be ready. The show was the same day as Emery and Gryffin's six-month anniversary. He wanted to write another song for her as a gift. She loved the last one he had written, and it was her favorite one to hear him sing. Gryffin wanted this one to be better. He worked the rest of the day figuring out chords and lyrics to Emery's song.

That night, Marcus came home. Gryffin awoke to the door opening and shutting. He walked out of his room to see Marcus opening up the fridge, looking for something to eat.

"Where have you been? You know I tried calling you?" Gryffin tried not to nag, but it was unsuccessful. He had been worrying about his brother all day.

"I got your messages," Marcus said without facing him.

"Where did you go? What did you do?" He sounded more and more like a parent.

"I didn't go get high if that's what you're implying," Marcus said, annoyed.

"Okay, then what happened?" Gryffin thought he still deserved an explanation.

Marcus's shoulders moved up and back down as he took a deep breath. He turned so that Gryffin could see him. In the pale refrigerator light, Gryffin could see a large cut running up the side of Marcus's face.

"What happened to you?" Gryffin rushed over to get a better look.

His face was bruised and bloodied, and one eye was swollen shut. Marcus said nothing.

"Did Dominic do this?" Gryffin asked, enraged. "Did he do this?"

Marcus made no noise and no motion. Gryffin spun on his heel and grabbed his keys from the counter, going to the door.

"Gryff, where are you going!" Marcus called after him.

"No one hurts my family," Gryffin asserted as he slammed the door.

Gryffin had been with Marcus while he was high so many times that he knew exactly where to find Dominic. Marcus would babble about the building under the bridge that always gave him such a kick. He was too out of it to know that he was giving Gryffin Dominic's exact location. At least that was what Gryffin thought. Even if Dominic wasn't there, he would keep looking for him. He wouldn't stop until he found him and made him pay for what he did to his brother.

Marcus's description of the place where he got his drugs was spot on. Underneath a bridge that covered a decent stretch of water was a broken-down stone building that looked to be abandoned for years. It wasn't though. As Gryffin pulled up to it, he saw multiple cars parked there and lights coming from the windows. When he walked up to the building, he could hear mellow music playing and people talking strangely. Gryffin thought about knocking but recognized it as a stupid idea. He was there to intimidate Dominic. What would knocking on the front door say about that?

Gryffin barged into the room like a charging horse. He saw about six people residing in the damp, foggy place. The room had random rugs lying on the ground, a few tables, and some chairs and couches that he assumed these people had found on the street and brought in. There were multiple lamps sitting on the floor and on the tables. Some had different colored lightbulbs, which explained why Gryffin thought there was a party going on before he entered the building. Everyone in the room looked at Gryffin as he barreled in, completely unfazed. They were the stereotypical stoners. Long, messy hair, loose clothing, and looking like they hadn't showered for days. There were packets of white stuff on one table and syringes with some vials on the other. Gryffin wasted no time.

"Where's Dominic?" Gryffin spoke with authority, like he had the right to be there.

A couple of them giggled drunkenly, and others just stared at him blankly.

"Who's asking?" a man sitting behind the table with the

syringes asked. He had long, dark hair and sported a thick beard. He wore a black, button-up shirt and dark dress pants with dress shoes. A gold watch was on his wrist, flaunting the money he must have. His eyes were unreadable, which didn't sit right with Gryffin.

"I am. Didn't you hear me?" Gryffin replied, unaware that that was probably not the ideal way to respond to a drug dealer.

The man chortled. "I'm Dominic. You're Marky's little brother, right?"

"Marcus," Gryffin corrected. "Does he owe you money? Is he using again?"

Dominic rose from his chair, revealing he was about as tall as Gryffin but much better built. He casually made his way to Gryffin. "No, he was specific about that. He didn't want any of my product. Just wanted to sell it for me."

"Sell it? Why would he do that? Marcus has a job already." Gryffin didn't follow.

"He got fired. What—he didn't tell you? Apparently the owner of the chain stopped in and recognized him from wandering the street when he was high. He was walked out, man. Came to me looking for some work, wanted to earn money quick. So I gave him a job."

Gryffin couldn't believe this. Marcus hadn't told him about losing his job or anything. "That still doesn't explain why my brother's all bloodied up."

"Your brother was late on a shipment. You see, he has one job—to pick up the drop-off and bring the package to me. We had to show him the consequences of not being punctual." Dominic spoke like a businessman. "He's paid extremely well for it, more than he should be. I like your brother. He's a decent guy—an idiot but still a good guy."

Gryffin punched Dominic square in the jaw. Dominic was caught off guard but didn't falter in his stance. He slowly turned back to him, cracking his jaw with his hand. "Good arm," he said as blood trickled from his lip.

"Leave him alone. Do you understand me?" Gryffin stood inches from Dominic's face, threatening him.

The stoners around them watched intently as if a play was being put on before them. They whispered to each other, not taking their eyes off of the men.

"You listen to me. Your brother is my employee now, whether you like it or not. He's doing this until I say he's free to leave. Until then, he works for me. So, man up and get over it. You'd do good to tell your brother that too." Dominic licked the blood off of his lip and spat at Gryffin. The blood splattered on Gryffin's face. He didn't flinch and wouldn't allow Dominic to intimidate him.

Dominic smiled darkly. "Get out of here, unless you want to be full of lead."

He nodded to another man who was sitting behind the table and was even bigger than Dominic. The man pulled out a Glock from behind his jacket and cocked it. Gryffin got the hint. He backed up to the door, not turning his back to Dominic. He felt the doorknob jab into his back, cueing him that he could quickly exit.

As he did, Dominic said, "Don't ever come back here."

Gryffin exited the building as fast as he could but also as calmly as he could. Dominic wouldn't see that he had frightened Gryffin. Honestly, Gryffin was more angry than afraid at that point. He knew going there would get Marcus in more trouble, and if Dominic already knew who Gryffin was, did he know about Emery? Gryffin stopped dead in his tracks at the thought of Dominic threatening Emery. Gryffin wouldn't allow anything to happen to her. He would put an end to Dominic's business; he wouldn't let Dominic terrorize their lives.

Chapter 17

"I'm not going to the police, Gryffin!" Marcus exclaimed.

Gryffin was pacing back and forth in the kitchen, trying to convince Marcus to go with him to the police station. "Why wouldn't you? He beat you up, and he's the number-one drug dealer in the city. How couldn't you want to put an end to that?" Gryffin was astonished that Marcus wasn't the least bit interested in getting back at Dominic.

"Dominic has eyes and ears everywhere, Gryff. I bet you he'd be out of jail as soon as he got in there," Marcus pointed out. "Even if he wasn't, his minions would continue his work."

Gryffin was so frustrated that he pounded his fist on the kitchen countertop. He ignored the stinging in his hand as he went back to pacing the room.

"We have to be smart and just do what he wants," Marcus stated.

"No way." Gryffin didn't even recognize his brother anymore.

"Marcus, you can't go back to working for that psychopath. You'll be providing more and more drug overdoses in the community, not to mention what you're doing is completely illegal. Marcus, why did you do this? Why didn't you just tell me you lost your job?"

"I was ashamed." Marcus looked at the floor with his good eye. "I didn't want to keep disappointing you. I wanted to show you I could take care of myself."

Gryffin knew Marcus meant every word. He sat down next to Gryffin on the couch and patted him on the back. "Man, I just want you to be okay. This, what you're doing, isn't. I would have helped you find another job if you would have just said something."

"I know." Marcus's voice quivered. There was nothing he could say that would express how sorry he was to Gryffin.

"I can't risk Emery getting in the crossfire, Marcus. Please come with me to the police."

"Did you not hear what I just said?" Marcus shot up from his seat to make a point. "It doesn't matter if Dominic does or doesn't go to jail; we'll be in danger. *All* of us."

Gryffin got up and stood inches from Marcus. "I will not put Emery in danger for a mistake that *you* made."

"The worst thing you can do is go to the police."

"Why? Because you might get into trouble too?" Gryffin understood why his brother was so against the idea now.

"I won't go to jail, Gryff," Marcus warned .

"So you'd rather put your brother and his girlfriend in immediate danger at all times?" Gryffin was appalled at Marcus's selfishness. "And what happens when you screw up again? You think he'll just beat you to a pulp next time? It could be Emery or me." He had nothing more to say to him. Sheer disbelief overcame

Gryffin. He shook his head. "You haven't changed. You're still a coward," Gryffin muttered as he went into his room, slamming the door.

Marcus stood alone in the living room. Gryffin was right. What he was doing wasn't right; he was being cowardly. He had to protect his family, especially after the car accident. Marcus wouldn't be the cause of another tragedy in his family. He loved his brother. In Marcus's own depraved way, he believed he was protecting Gryffin by not going to the police. But the more he thought about it, he knew Gryffin was right. He would have to go to the police sooner or later, even if that meant being arrested himself.

Emery got off of work early and decided to drop by Gryffin's apartment to see if he wanted to go to dinner. She walked up to apartment 316 and knocked on the door three times. While she waited, Emery brushed out the wrinkles in her blouse from sitting in the car. She still got nervous every time she went to see Gryffin, and she wanted to look perfect for him. It didn't matter though; Gryffin thought she was beautiful in sweatpants and without makeup. Still, she wanted to look her very best for him.

The handle turned, and the door cracked open. Gryffin stood on the other side, only half of him visible. "Emery, what are you doing here?" He sounded like he was accusing her of something.

Emery took no notice. "I didn't have any more clients today, so I thought I would see if you wanted to grab a bite to eat. There's this special at The Lift that we—"

"No," Gryffin interrupted. "I can't tonight."

This was unlike Gryffin. "Oh." Emery's hopes had been extinguished. She noticed something strange about Gryffin. It was his eyes. They were distant and not in the daydreaming way. "Is everything okay?" Emery asked.

"Yeah, great," Gryffin said shallowly with a smile.

Emery knew he was trying to get rid of her. "Okay, then. Did you want to get together tomorrow?" She tried to give him the benefit of the doubt. Maybe he was busy practicing or something.

"I'm busy then too," Gryffin replied, not making eye contact with her.

"Do you have a show coming up or something? Because you'll be great. You don't have to worry about—"

"I'm fine, Emery," Gryffin abruptly cut in.

There was silence between them for a moment. Emery had never seen Gryffin like this before—far off and uninviting. He was blocking her out, but why? Emery tried not to take it personally, but she couldn't help it. Was he mad at *her*? Not much made Gryffin upset other than his brother. Maybe that was the problem. Whatever it was, Emery wasn't going to get it out of him.

"I need to go. I'll call you." Gryffin turned from her and shut the door.

"Right," Emery got out before the door shut in her face. She stood there for another minute before leaving, waiting to see if he would come out and explain what in the world was going on with him. But he didn't. Emery decided he just needed space. She went back to her car and drove away.

Gryffin watched her from his bedroom window until she left. He didn't want to give her the cold shoulder, but what else could he do? If Dominic saw her with him, she would become leverage. The thought of Dominic getting his disgusting hands on her infuriated Gryffin. He would not allow that to happen. He put his head in his hands, not knowing the next time he would be able to see Emery.

Gryffin dodged Emery's calls and texts for two weeks. She had shown up to his apartment multiple times as well, but no luck. Sometimes Marcus would answer the door and say Gryffin wasn't home, and other times no one would answer. Emery knew he wanted to be alone, but she couldn't handle the radio silence. Still, she wasn't going to go out of her way to see him. This was ending up like another bad breakup, and she was not going to give Gryffin the upper hand. She decided to go back to Gryffin's apartment once more and not take no for an answer.

Emery pulled up to the apartment complex that Gryffin was staying in. She didn't see his car parked in the street where it would have been if he were home. Emery parked in his spot and made her way to Gryffin's apartment. She took a small breath before knocking on the door three times. Footsteps were heard on the other side of the door, coming closer. Then the lock clicked, and the handle turned. Marcus answered the door again.

"Emery, hi. Gryffin isn't here."

"I know. I saw that when I pulled up," Emery confirmed.

"Did you need something?" Marcus didn't know why she would bother coming up to the apartment if she knew Gryffin wasn't there.

"I actually wanted to talk to you," Emery said. Marcus wasn't her first pick to talk to, but she saw no other choice.

"Okay, come in." Marcus opened the door wider.

Emery fiddled with her hands, unsure of how to start. Marcus closed the door and watched her nervous habit. He crossed his arms. "Are you okay?"

"Yes, I mean, I don't know. I guess I'm confused and don't really know who else to talk to," Emery answered honestly.

"Gryffin still hasn't talked to you, I take it." Marcus pieced it together.

"Yeah. I'm sorry. I just don't know what's going on, and you're his brother, so I thought you would maybe know what was happening with him, and now I'm just rambling." Emery remembered to breathe. She didn't want to put Marcus in this position; it wasn't fair to him.

"Emery, it's okay. Gryffin has just been busy with the band and helping me with finding a new job."

"What happened to the gas station?"

"Yeah, well, it didn't work out the way I had hoped."

"I'm sorry, Marcus. I know that job was a big step for you." Emery felt bad for him; she knew how hard he worked. She hoped this didn't turn him back to his old ways. That would explain Gryffin's behavior. Marcus wasn't acting off though; he actually looked better than he had in the past two weeks.

"It's okay. It's just a job. There are plenty of those." Marcus acted as if it was no big deal for him. "Anyway, Gryffin has just been busy." He didn't want to tell Emery the real reason—that he was in with a ruthless drug lord, and if he messed up again, he could potentially get her and Gryffin hurt or worse. Marcus decided to give as little detail as possible without lying to Emery. "Just give him some more time."

"That's the thing. I have. It's been two weeks, Marcus. Two weeks without talking to me or knowing how he is. We haven't been together long, but I really care about him. He's my best friend. I miss him."

This hit Marcus like a ton of concrete. It wasn't Gryffin that was hurting Emery; it was him. He walked over to the other side of the living room, contemplating his next move. He knew how much Gryffin cared for Emery, and he couldn't keep them apart. Marcus knew it was time for this to end. He turned back to Emery, who anxiously waited for him to say something.

"Do you want to stay for dinner?" he asked.

Surprised, Emery didn't see why not. "Okay, yeah. Thank you."

"I'm not much of a cook, but I do think there's a frozen pizza I can bake." Marcus walked into the kitchen and opened the freezer.

"Okay." Emery didn't know what was happening. She decided to just go with it. Maybe this was a good chance to get to know Marcus—the real Marcus and not the version Gryffin made him out to be.

As Marcus readied the cheap frozen pizza on a pan and set the oven for the right temperature, he hoped his plan would work. He would try to keep Emery there for as long as he could. It was getting late, and Gryffin had to come home sometime.

Chapter 18

At ten thirty, the front door to the Brooks' apartment un-locked from the outside and opened. Marcus and Emery had been having a lovely time together. They ate a sausage and pepperoni pizza that Marcus had baked in the oven and talked for a few hours. The subjects they had touched were everything from movies to politics. Marcus could see why Gryffin liked Emery so much. She was a great communicator. Because Marcus was quite guarded about his personal life, as was Emery, they found it easier to talk to each other. It wasn't awkward, and there weren't any pauses where they didn't know how to pick up another conversation. Emery found that they had the same sense of humor. Sarcasm and blatant jokes were their strong suits. Gryffin walked in as they were sharing a laugh about a line in a movie they had both seen and thought was hilarious.

Gryffin stopped dead in his tracks; Emery was the last person he had expected to see. He was so happy to see her though. She looked more beautiful to him now than ever, and he had missed her so much. But Gryffin kept his cool; he had to pretend like he wasn't thrilled she was there. Then she would think she could stay. Then Dominic could find her. Gryffin couldn't put her in harm's way.

"Gryff, there you are." Marcus smiled, hiding his intention of trying to smooth things over between them. "Where were you?"

"Derek's," he answered bluntly.

"Right." Marcus could see the plan was not off to a good start. He motioned to Emery. "Well, Emery stopped by to say hello. You weren't here, so I invited her to stay for dinner."

"I see." Gryffin didn't look at Emery. He couldn't.

Emery waited for Gryffin to say something to her. He didn't. Not even a hello.

Marcus could sense the tension. He stood up from his chair and began to walk to Gryffin's room. "I'm just going to work on my resume. We left some pizza out for you if you're hungry."

"I'm not." Gryffin kept his eyes on Marcus.

"Okay, well if you do get hungry, it's there." Marcus gave a small nod in Emery's direction, showing Gryffin that they needed to talk about what was happening. "Good night, Emery." He waved.

"Good night. Thank you for dinner." She waved back.

"No problem. Come back anytime." He smiled and closed the bedroom door behind him.

Gryffin and Emery stood in the kitchen alone.

Several uncomfortable seconds passed. Gryffin averted his eyes from her, guilt sweeping over him. Emery noticed this instantly; he wasn't himself. He was usually ecstatic to see her. But right here and now, he seemed like he'd rather be anywhere but there.

Emery cleared her throat to give Gryffin a chance to start the conversation. When he didn't, Emery said, "So, how are you?"

"I'm fine," Gryffin answered quickly without thinking. He clenched his jaw, knowing how rude that must have sounded to her.

"Oh, that's good." Emery tried to move past the abrupt reply. "I tried calling you. I left messages."

"I got them."

Emery was trying to not take his harshness personally; this was not at all like Gryffin. She just wanted to know what was going on. Maybe she could help him through whatever he was dealing with. Emery needed to get to the bottom of all of this uncertainty. She straightened up. "What's going on with you, Gryffin? You haven't spoken to me in two weeks, and you just left me out on your doorstep with no explanation as to why you're being so cold." Emery's default rationalization was that she was the cause of this mess. After all, with everyone else she had been involved with, it seemed to always be her fault. "What did I do?"

Gryffin's eyes finally met Emery's. Sadness and insecurity were painted on his face. "You did nothing wrong, Em." The last thing Gryffin wanted was for Emery to feel like she was responsible for his behavior.

"Then tell me what's happening." She took a step closer to him. "Please, Gryffin. You've always told me that I need to let my guard down, that I need to let people in. I can't," she paused, "I can't take you freezing me out like this. I care about you, and I want to help you. Let *me* in, Gryffin."

Gryffin felt a jab in his stomach. Guilt and resentment for his actions cut through him. "I can't," was all he managed to get out.

"You can't or you won't?"

Gryffin opened up the cabinet door and took out a glass. He filled it with water from the sink and took a drink. Emery knew he was closing up on her once again. She would not allow it this time.

"Gryffin, I know your brother's dealing with some things, okay? I know he's a recovering addict, and I know he's unstable, but tonight I really got to know him. I got to see him for who he is, and he's not a bad person. He may be a little lost, but I can tell he's trying hard to be a better person. So you don't have to put on this act to get me to stay away from you so I won't see him. You don't have to protect me from Marcus."

Gryffin slammed down his glass on the countertop, the noise startling Emery. He spun around to face her, frustration kicking in. "I'm not protecting you from Marcus, Emery! I'm protecting you from someone much worse!"

"What do you mean?" Emery was frightened by Gryffin's outburst.

He took a breath, lowering his voice. "Marcus is working for a really bad guy, Emery. I tried to get him out of it, but I can't. If Marcus messes up this job or goes to the police about it ..." Gryffin shook his head. "Then I become a target. Which means you could become one too."

"He's back working for his dealer, isn't he?" Emery could see the clear picture now.

Gryffin nodded. "I can't let anything happen to you. I'm not ... I'm strong enough to protect you. This is the only way I know how. If you stay away, he has no way of knowing you and I are connected. I need you to be safe."

Everything made sense. The unanswered texts, the voicemails

that he never got back to, the visits where Marcus claimed Gryffin wasn't there. He was trying to keep Emery out of danger.

Gryffin ran his fingers through his hair and leaned on the dining room table, composing himself. Without warning, he locked with her and said, "I love you, Emery."

Emery's world stopped. She couldn't think. She couldn't breathe. She couldn't move. The words hit her like a wave crashing into the sea. Only this didn't hurt. It felt like relief. Like everything in her entire life didn't seem as important. She didn't have to work for these words; she only had to be herself. That's how Emery knew what Gryffin spoke was completely and irrefutably true.

Gryffin crossed his arms, protecting himself from what Emery's response might be. He didn't blame her for being mad at him for acting so cold to her. He would even understand if she wanted to end it then and there. All of those thoughts were silenced with one gesture. Emery cocked her head to the side, looking him over. Not judgmentally though; it was more of a realization of something that had been there all along. She came closer to him and wrapped her arms around him, holding him tightly. Gryffin let loose his arms and hugged her back. He had no way to fight her, and he didn't want to. The only thing he wanted was to be with Emery right in that moment and nowhere else.

"I love you too, Gryffin," Emery said quietly. "I forgive you."

Gryffin tightened his arms around Emery's back, holding her closer. He buried his face in her shoulder so she wouldn't see one stray tear fall from his eye and roll down his cheek.

Emery knew Gryffin's intentions were good and he was truly sorry. That was all she needed. Everything she needed was there with him.

"We're going to figure this out," she reassured him, "but we have to do it together."

Gryffin knew she was right. His mind continued to go back to Dominic's threat. If anything happened to Emery because of Gryffin, he couldn't live with himself. In this time they had though, Gryffin didn't want to think about Dominic or Marcus. He didn't want to make a plan or figure out a way to secure Emery's safety. Gryffin just wanted to make this moment last for as long as possible.

"Can we just be here right now? Just for a few minutes?" he asked her, his head resting on hers now.

Emery tilted her head up so their eyes met. "However long you need."

Gryffin lightly kissed Emery's forehead. Emery laid her head under his chin, listening to his heartbeat. This moment would be in their hearts for a lifetime.

Chapter 19

*E*ven though Emery had every right to drag out Gryffin's groveling for ignoring her over the past two weeks, she let it go. This was why Gryffin loved her. She didn't hold a grudge; if anything, she wanted to understand and help him in any way she could. The thought of Emery being on Dominic's radar still bothered Gryffin. He was convinced there had to be a way to ensure her safety without pushing her away. Dominic probably could be bought, but Gryffin knew he would ask for an unreasonable amount of money. That was out of the question. Marcus was the only answer, and Gryffin knew it. Gryffin hated it. He didn't want his brother handling dirty work for Dominic; he had been clean for so long, and just being around the stuff could get him hooked again. For now, Gryffin was at an impasse.

Gryffin and Emery slowly started to go back to their old ways. After band rehearsal, Gryffin would drive around Emery's block a couple times to make sure no one was tailing him. Even after that, he would park a block away from her apartment and walk in case someone were to find his car. This went on for a little over three weeks. It was ridiculous to Gryffin that he wasn't able to take his girlfriend out to dinner or even take a walk in the park. They were restricted to her apartment, and they were going crazy.

One night, Emery had just about had enough of the feeling of confinement. She stood up from her sofa, in the middle of an old movie that she and Gryffin were watching on television, and took Gryffin by the hand.

"What are you doing?" Gryffin was actually pretty into this black-and-white film.

"Come on, we're getting out of here." Emery pulled a reluctant Gryffin to his feet.

"Em, you know that isn't a good idea. Dominic could have someone watching us. It isn't safe for us to be seen together." Gryffin plopped back down on the couch.

"It's been almost a month and nothing. If you ask me, you've been watching too many of these gangster movies and are a little too paranoid."

"Look, I'd rather spend a quiet evening cooped up in your apartment than out on the town putting you in harm's way." Gryffin gave a half smile. "As long as I'm with you, I don't care what we do."

Emery rolled her eyes. "Well I care that we've been here loafing while the world around us passes by. You were the one who wanted me to try new things and experience life to the fullest." She prodded at him, "I think you've lost your touch."

"No, no, no." Gryffin wagged his finger at her. "I'm just being smart."

"Yeah and playing it safe," Emery said under her breath.

Gryffin's eyes narrowed. "Fine, okay, you want to go out? We'll go out." Gryffin clicked the remote control to turn off the television and stood up. "Where to, Miss Everett?" He tossed the remote back on the couch and folded his hands like a child waiting for a piece of candy.

"I'll drive." Emery winked.

Emery pulled into the parking lot of The Lift and was able to find a spot just beside a lamppost. That way it would be easy to remember when she came out to find her car later. It was Friday night, and the crowd would be coming soon to see the band The Lift was showcasing tonight. Gryffin and Emery hopped out of her small car and walked hand in hand up to the restaurant. Inside, there was still a good amount of people who were eating, without all of the usual Friday night bandies. Emery and Gryffin waited to be seated, people watching as they did so. Gryffin hoped they could stay for the live entertainment; he enjoyed watching other local artists perform. Of course, because it was Friday night at The Lift, Gryffin and Emery were forced to sit at the bar once again. It was fine with Emery; it brought a rush of sentiment from when she and Gryffin had first met. She wondered if he felt the same about it.

Gryffin and Emery ordered their meals—Emery's usual chicken salad with tea, and Gryffin ordered a hamburger with a soda. Even though it wasn't his idea, Gryffin was glad that they had gotten out of Emery's apartment. Emery had surprised him with her impulsiveness. She hadn't stepped outside of her normality alone before this, so it was a big step for Emery in coming out of her shell. What Gryffin loved the most about this was that he was a part of it.

"Here you two go." The bartender slid Gryffin and Emery's steaming plates of food before them. "Enjoy."

They thanked the bartender. Emery noticed that it was the same bartender from the night they met. Everything seemed to be coming full circle. Before Emery could take the first bite of her meal, Gryffin raised his glass.

"A toast," Gryffin said, "to pushing boundaries and living dangerously." He was half-joking.

Emery lifted her glass and clinked it against his. "You're welcome," she teased back. She took a drink of her sweet tea.

Gryffin scoffed before taking a sip of his own beverage. The two ate and talked like they had done many times before. They never seemed to run out of things to talk about. Gryffin could listen to Emery for hours, which he had. Emery loved the way Gryffin could tell stories. She guessed he was so good at it because he was a songwriter, which made her remember something she had wanted to ask him a while ago.

"So you know that song you wrote?" Emery began.

"Which one?" Gryffin had written many songs, but he was certain that he knew which one she was talking about.

"You know, the one you sang for me at your concert."

"Oh, *that* song. Your song." Gryffin smiled broadly.

"Yes, that one. Do you have a copy of it or something? I'd really love to have one." Emery felt a bit embarrassed asking for something sentimental. She had never cared for that sort of thing before. But now everything was different. Gryffin was different.

"I think I have one I could give to you," Gryffin said snootily like he was too good to give her one.

"If it's not too much trouble." She knew he was messing with her. "I know you big, brooding musicians like to keep all of your original material for yourself."

Gryffin pointed at Emery with his index finger. "You can never be too careful. If a song like that got into the wrong hands, you would be theirs instantly." He took a big bite of his sandwich.

"Not necessarily." Emery shook her head. "You wouldn't be singing it, so it wouldn't mean anything to me anyway." She averted her eyes after saying that. *When did I get so sappy?* She plunged her fork into a piece of chicken salad and ate it.

With a mouthful of burger, Gryffin smiled a toothless smile, his cheeks bulging with the large amount of food he had shoveled in moments before. As he finished chewing, he watched Emery uncomfortably fork the rest of her food and scarf it down. Emery was never one for romanticism; that was always Gryffin's mind-set. Another milestone was in the making for Emery's pessimistic personality lift.

When Gryffin's mouth was clear of sandwich remnants, he said, "It will always be my song to you, Miss Everett. No matter who sings it."

Emery's cheeks flushed a little as she looked back at Gryffin. "Good to know."

Just then, the announcer for the performance portion of the evening walked up on stage and grabbed the microphone. "Good evening, everyone! Are you all ready for another night of music?"

The crowd cheered. Emery realized that while she and Gryffin had eaten their meal, more people had made their way in and gathered in front of the stage. A decent amount of people were there but not nearly as many as Escalates brought in when they played here. Gryffin clapped and yelled, feeding the atmosphere of excitement for the special entertainment.

"Fantastic! It is my pleasure to introduce," he pointed stage right, "the Lightning Round!" He clapped for the band as he walked down the front end of the stage and disappeared into the crowd. The people around the stage erupted in shouts and more clapping. The band, Lightning Round, came on stage, tongues out and fists thrusts in the air. There were four of them, and they all looked exactly the same—hardcore rock and rollers. Long, stringy hair fell beyond their shoulders, piercings in their ears, and tattoos all over every visible part of their bodies. The band said nothing to the audience; instead, they plugged in their instruments, or sat in behind the drum set, and went right into their first song. Emery couldn't explain what the song was like except that it was loud. Terribly loud. The lead singer began screaming lyrics, and Emery was over it instantaneously. They had talent, no doubt, but this style of music was not to Emery's liking. Gryffin wasn't much of a fan either, but he made the most of it. He started head banging and throwing up a rock fist as the song kept going. Emery laughed at him while he did this. He stood up next to her and took her hands, bringing her to her feet. He started jumping up and down like a rabbit and shaking his rock star hair back and forth, encouraging Emery to join him. She was reluctant at first, worrying about what people would think. Eighty percent of them were acting as wild as Gryffin was, and some were even worse. But as always, Emery gave in. She danced crazily with Gryffin along to the inaudible lyrics the lead singer was blasting into the mic. Emery had never laughed so hard in her entire life. When Emery broke into a giggling frenzy, Gryffin couldn't contain himself either. The two danced, jumped, and laughed the entire song, not caring about anyone who looked at them as lunatics.

The first song ended, and Emery had to catch her breath. She steadied herself by leaning into Gryffin's chest, gasping for air. The look Emery had on her face was priceless to Gryffin. Pure joy. The dimples in her cheeks were visible, something Gryffin hadn't noticed before that night. Her eyes were watery from the laughter, but they were also very much alive. Gryffin took advantage of the moment at hand. He cupped his hands on both sides of her face and leaned in, kissing her gently. Emery had no time to react. And yet she gave into Gryffin, wrapping her arms around his neck and kissing him back. It was times like these when Gryffin knew that Emery was the one person he wanted to share his life with. One day, he planned to.

When they pulled back from each other but were still in each other's arms, Emery smiled and wrinkled her nose. Gryffin thought this was the absolute most adorable thing in the entire world. Moments like this mattered most to him, and he knew that right then and there.

Out of the corner of Emery's eye, she spotted Marcus. He was slumped up in a booth in the darkest and furthest part of The Lift with a man Emery didn't know. She nodded in their direction. "What's Marcus doing here?"

Gryffin looked in the direction Emery motioned him to. There was Marcus, dressed in dark colors, a serious expression on his face. The man Marcus was with was bigger than him and dressed nicer. His hair was slicked back, and his shirtsleeves were rolled up to his elbows as if he were hard at work. "I don't know." Gryffin hoped that the man Marcus was with wasn't working for Dominic. Gryffin put a hand on Emery's back and walked her back to the bar protectively, watching Marcus and the stranger as he did so.

"Do you think they're watching us?" Emery tried not to sound worried.

"No, I don't think so. They haven't looked over at us once. Plus the place is packed, so I doubt they could have kept a good eye on us anyway," Gryffin observed.

"What do we do?" Emery asked.

Gryffin surveyed the situation. They could leave and risk being seen beyond the crowd. Or they could stay, nestled on the other side of the large audience, and watch Marcus from afar. "Let's just lay low here for a little bit."

"What if they see us?"

"I don't think they will. If we stay back here, we should be okay." Gryffin kept his focus on Marcus.

Emery sensed an ulterior motive. "You're going to spy on him, aren't you?"

"Not spy. I just want to see what he's up to." Gryffin knew that was the definition of spying.

"Okay, I'm in." Emery turned from the bar and in the direction of Marcus.

"You don't mind?"

"Of course not. I care about Marcus too. I don't want him getting into trouble any more than you do," Emery stated as she watched Marcus from across the room.

Gryffin liked this side of Emery. But he had to be reasonable. "Okay. But we'll only stay for a little longer. If nothing happens, we'll go. Deal?"

"Deal." Emery nodded.

The first twenty minutes, Marcus and the stranger didn't move. They didn't even speak. The men sat in silence, not looking at each other. Their gazes would drift to the metal band that was still performing on stage, and then they would stare back into the nothingness. Gryffin and Emery took turns looking over their shoulders in Marcus's direction to see if any change had ensued. This way they were less likely to be noticed for full-on watching them with their entire bodies turned from the other side of the room. Finally, the stranger moved.

"Hey, something's happening." Emery spoke quietly. She turned back to the bar.

Gryffin slightly turned his bar stool to his left, taking his glass in hand and casually sipping from it. He darted his eyes to Marcus and the stranger. The stranger seemed to be on the phone with someone. Marcus looked to be listening intently from the other side of the table, as if awaiting instruction. Then, all at once, the two men got up from their seats and made their way through the crowd toward Gryffin and Emery.

"Oh no." Gryffin swiveled back to face the bar. He set his soda on the counter, trying to decide if a better plan would be to book it out of the restaurant or stay and risk the confrontation. He gave Emery an urgent look. "Don't move, okay? Keep your head down and don't turn around."

"Why? What's wrong?" Emery's eyes could not hide her fright.

"They're coming this way. If they ask me who you are, I'll just say you're a stranger. Someone I had to sit next to at the bar because all the other seats were taken. Just act like you don't know me."

Emery didn't like the sound of that. This was the only plan they had though, and if Gryffin thought it was best, then she would do it without question.

Marcus and the stranger pushed through the rowdy crowd of metal heads and were almost upon Gryffin and Emery. Gryffin ran his story over and over in the seconds he had before they reached him. He was there to listen to the local band, and if they asked who Emery was, the place was crowded, and he was forced to sit there. The thought of having to act like Emery was nothing to him made Gryffin cringe. She was everything to him. But if disowning her in front of her brother and Dominic's thug would throw them off the scent, then he would have to stomach the feeling for her benefit.

Gryffin took a deep breath. Marcus and the stranger were only a few feet away from them. He got ready to act surprised to see them there, but then they turned right and walked to the front of the room by the stage. Gryffin let out a breath of relief. Marcus and the stranger hadn't come to watch them. In fact, he was sure that they didn't see Gryffin or Emery at all.

"They're gone." Gryffin let Emery know she could relax.

"They're gone?" Emery looked to the empty darkened booth where the men had been sitting. "They didn't see us?"

Gryffin shook his head. "No, they didn't. They came for something though."

He watched Marcus and the stranger go to the back of The Lift and to the alleyway door next to the stage. The stranger went through it first. Before Marcus followed, he took a last glance around the restaurant. Then he went out the alley door, closing it behind him.

"I'll be right back," Gryffin said as he got up from his stool.

"Wait, Gryffin." Emery knew he was going after his brother. She wanted to help, and she didn't want him walking into some unknown trouble behind that door.

"Stay here, Emery. I'll be right back." He touched her shoulder, reassuring her.

Emery knew she couldn't stop him. She had no right to. So she gave Gryffin an unconvincing smile and watched him go out the door. She prayed she would see him walk back through it soon.

Chapter 20

The alley beside The Lift was just that, a poorly paved, gravel-filled path between The Lift and another brick building beside it. It was evening outside, making Gryffin rely on the lights that were mounted over the doorway to The Lift and the streetlights that stood at the beginning and the end of the alley. Gryffin exited through the alley door cautiously; he didn't want to draw attention to himself. He only wanted to see what Marcus was up to. As Marcus's brother, it was Gryffin's obligation to look out for him, even when he wasn't wanted. Gryffin turned his head to the left, peering down the alley. Nothing but a dumpster and a few trash cans. Then he turned to his right. About twenty feet from him, Gryffin could make out two dark figures walking away from him. He moved swiftly to keep up with them, keeping to the shadows and trying his best not to make any noise. *What are they doing out here?*

When the two figures reached the end of the alley, they

stopped. Gryffin stopped too and leaned up against the building to keep out of their line of sight. To his advantage, the alley was not lit well. They would have to shine a flashlight directly on Gryffin to be able to make out his shape. Gryffin watched them for a few minutes. They stood there in the middle of the alley, not talking. The stranger lit a cigarette. After he blew out smoke, he offered it to Marcus. To Gryffin's surprise, Marcus put out a hand and declined. The stranger shrugged and continued to smoke the cigarette. Was this all they came out here for? To have a smoke break? Gryffin didn't see the point in Marcus coming outside just for that, especially when he wasn't going to partake in the inhaling of tobacco.

Just then, a large black Hummer pulled into the entrance of the alley where Marcus and the stranger stood. The Hummer stopped a few feet in front of them, the headlights igniting the entirety of the alley. Gryffin hoped they still weren't able to see him. They hadn't yet. They didn't even turn his way. The front driver's-side door opened. The car was still running, so Gryffin assumed that whatever it was they were about to do wasn't going to take long. He continued to watch with his back flat against the side of The Lift.

The man who got out of the Hummer was tall and brawny. He wore a black leather coat, dark jeans, and combat boots. His hair was shorter than the stranger with Marcus, but it was slicked back the same way. He was cleanly shaven and had hoops in his ears. The man shut the car door and came around to the front of the vehicle. He tossed his cigarette on the ground and stomped it out. He nodded to Marcus and the stranger.

"Good to see you, Kyle." He shook the stranger's hand. The stranger named Kyle didn't say anything back; he just nodded in agreement. The man gave Marcus a judgmental face, looking him up and down and not seeming impressed. "You Dominic's new boy?"

"I am," Marcus replied. Gryffin could tell from Marcus's voice that he was putting on a brave face. "Marcus." He extended his hand to the man.

The man's eyes went from Marcus to Kyle and back to Marcus. He raised his eyebrows. "Right." He ignored Marcus's gesture. "This is the last job you have with a partner, right? I mean, you don't have to be babysat anymore because of your last incident?"

"That's right," Marcus said.

"Okay then, let's get to it. Shall we?" Charles turned on his heel and walked to the back of the Hummer. He came back with a large metal briefcase. Charles set it on the hood of the Hummer and took out a key from his pocket. He put the small key in the lock and turned it to the right, clicking the case open. Charles pushed up the lid, opening the case wide enough for Marcus and Kyle to see what its contents were. Gryffin couldn't see because of the headlights.

"Gentlemen, a new supply for Dominic, as promised." Charles walked over to Marcus. "And my payment?"

Kyle motioned to Marcus, who retrieved a large brown envelope from his left inside jacket pocket. He handed the weighty package to Charles. "It's all there. I counted it myself."

"You've had mishaps before. I'll just count it again to make sure." Charles plopped the envelope on the hood next to the briefcase. He counted one by one the bills Marcus had delivered to him. They stood awkwardly, waiting for him to finish. When he was satisfied with the amount he counted out, Charles smiled. He put the money back into the envelope and tucked it away in his jacket pocket. Charles then closed the briefcase, locking it back up. He held out the key to Marcus. "See? It's really not a hard job, is it?"

Marcus took the key hastily. Gryffin couldn't believe he had just witnessed a drug deal involving his brother. Fury and disappointment coursed through him. Charles patted Marcus on the back as a sign of a job well done. Suddenly his face turned from contentment to deadly.

"You! Right there!" Charles yelled, stomping over to Gryffin.

Gryffin was found out. He couldn't run. Charles knew what he looked like, so he would find him anyway. Gryffin did the only thing that seemed logical at the time: he stayed to fight.

"Who are you?" Charles snarled inches from Gryffin's face.

Gryffin didn't answer. He stared at Charles with a furrowed brow.

Charles got closer to Gryffin. "What did you see?"

"Nothing. Well, except the drug deal that just happened right in front of me a few seconds ago. Nothing spectacular," Gryffin said abruptly and unafraid.

"Who do you work for?" Charles automatically drew a speculation that Gryffin was a nark.

"Myself mostly. But I'm more of a man of the people." Gryffin grinned widely.

Charles crumpled up Gryffin's shirt collar with his fists, pushing him against the wall.

"I'm going to ask you again." His patience was thin now. "Who. Are. You?" He spoke slowly, as if Gryffin was incompetent.

"I'm just a musician," Gryffin answered cockily. He wasn't going to give into Charles's threatening gestures.

"A musician, huh?" He laughed. Charles let go of his shirt and took a small step back, amused with Gryffin. He thrust his fist into Gryffin's ribcage, knocking the wind out of him.

Gryffin gasped, doubled over in pain. Charles grabbed Gryffin's hair and yanked his head up to eye level. "Then let's hear you sing." With that, Charles did a jab to the right side of Gryffin's face. Gryffin's head whipped to the left, so Charles beat it back to the right.

By this time, Kyle and Marcus had come to see what the commotion was.

"What's going on here?" Kyle's voice boomed. It was deep and bellowed over the scuffle.

Charles socked Gryffin in the jaw one more time before giving him an answer. He pointed to Gryffin. "He saw us!"

"Who is he?" Kyle asked.

"I don't know. He won't tell me! But we can't let him go, man. He could tell someone, and we would be finished!" Charles said.

Marcus hadn't gotten a good look at the spy. He was crowded by Kyle and the infuriated Charles. Marcus took a step into the madness to see who this person was. He saw his only brother, crumpled on the ground. His lip was bleeding, and his face was bruised.

"Gryff?" Marcus was horrified by the sight.

Kyle and Charles's heads snapped in Marcus's direction. "*You* know him?" Kyle questioned.

Marcus's eyes were welling. "He's my brother." There was no

point in lying to these men. They would figure out who Gryffin was eventually, and that would end worse for everyone.

Charles scoffed, "Really?" He was excited by this. "So we have a little family reunion going on."

"Look, I'm sure he won't tell anyone about tonight. You can trust him. Right, Gryffin?"

Gryffin remained silent. He spat out a mix of saliva and blood to the side of him.

Marcus waited for a response. "Right?"

Still no answer.

Marcus decided to take a different route, "You have *my* word."

"Normally I would believe that. I would trust that you would make sure this remained between us. But," he shrugged, "with your little mishap a short while ago, I can't take any chances." Charles pulled a gun out from under his coat. He held it out to Marcus, hilt up. "You have to take care of this, Marcus."

Marcus's eyes were wide with fear. "You want me to kill my brother?"

"Kill? No!" Charles chuckled darkly. "I don't want you to kill him. I just want you to send him a message."

"What kind of message?" Marcus didn't understand.

"That you are not to be toyed with. You are in control here, not him. And he will do what you tell him to if he knows what's good for him." Charles held the gun hilt higher to Marcus. "Think of it as your final task to get Dominic's full trust back. Just a shot in the leg will do."

Marcus stood frozen. If he didn't do this, Marcus was certain that Charles would kill Gryffin. If he did, the relationship he had with Gryffin would be severed forever. Gryffin wouldn't be dead though. He would be able to have a life with Emery. Marcus just wanted Gryffin to be happy, even if that meant he wasn't a part of his brother's life anymore. Marcus shakily took the gun from Charles's grasp. He aimed at Gryffin's lower right leg. Anxiety and total terror overtook him. He was going to close his eyes. Marcus couldn't bear to watch as he hurt his brother. He was just about to clamp his eyes shut when he truly looked at his brother—beaten and battered, tears and hopelessness in his eyes. Marcus took a deep breath and knew it was now or never. He shut his eyes and counted to three.

One … You can do this, Marcus. You have to save him. Two … They'll kill him if you don't. Just pull the trigger! Three …

Gryffin flinched.

He didn't feel anything. He opened his eyes.

Marcus was still standing there with the gun aimed at Gryffin's leg, but there was no wound. He didn't fire the gun.

"I won't," Marcus said.

"You won't?" Charles's face was scrunched up like he had just eaten something sour.

"No, I won't," Marcus repeated. "I'm not going to hurt my brother, Charles."

Inside, Gryffin smiled. A rush of relief and empathy ran over him. Marcus had stood up for him. His brother was back.

Charles ran his hands over his face in anguish. He had been disrespected by an errand boy. Charles put his hands on his hips and stared blankly at Marcus for a moment. Suddenly, he grabbed the gun from Marcus, pushing him back.

"You will regret your disobedience, boy!" he yelled.

Gryffin shot up from the ground and ran right into Charles, sacking him to the ground. He wrestled Charles for the gun, trying to get it out of his sinister hands. Kyle ran over to help Charles, grabbing Gryffin and trying to pull him off. Marcus came from behind Kyle and wrapped his arm around his neck, putting Kyle in a chokehold and forcing Marcus to let go of Gryffin. Gryffin hit Charles twice in the nose and once in the throat so he wouldn't focus all of his energy on keeping the gun in his grip. When Charles was trying to catch his breath from the throat jab, Gryffin hit Charles's hand hard against the cement, making the gun fall out of Charles's now loose fingers.

Kyle had broken out of Marcus's hold and head-butted him hard. Marcus fell to his knees, blood trickling from his forehead. Kyle, with his brute strength, lifted Marcus back to his feet and gave him a few uppercuts to his stomach. Gryffin saw that his brother needed him. Kicking the gun out of the discombobulated Charles's reach, Gryffin ran over to aid Marcus. He saw a trash can, which gave him an idea. Gryffin grabbed hold of the lid and ran at full speed to Kyle, ramming the tin lid hard into the side of his face. Kyle flopped onto his side, taken by surprise. He tried to get up, but when he did, Gryffin was waiting for him. Gryffin smacked the lid right across Kyle's face, knocking him out cold. The two brothers stood victorious amongst their enemies, who lay unconscious before them.

Marcus and Gryffin panted, recovering from their attackers. Gryffin was surprised that no one had heard the commotion. Then he remembered there was a metal band playing just on the other side of the wall. Marcus wiped the blood off of his forehead with the back of his hand.

"You okay?" Gryffin's breathing was still heavy.

"Yeah, Kyle just got a good hit in." He winced as he touched his wounded head. He took another breath. "I'm sorry. I shouldn't have taken that gun in the first place. But if I didn't, they would have killed you."

"I know you were just trying to do the lesser of two evils." Gryffin understood. He looked at the unconscious Kyle and Charles. "So what now?"

Marcus thought for a moment. He walked over to the briefcase and picked it up. "I'm going to take this to the police."

"Wait, they could trace this back to you," Gryffin rationalized. Then he understood. "You're going to turn yourself in."

"It's the only way to end all of this. Dominic will get arrested along with the rest of his minions. You'll be safe. Emery too," Marcus stated.

Gryffin couldn't believe his brother was going to give up his freedom for them. Every awful thought Gryffin had ever had about Marcus was revoked—replaced with respect. He walked over to his brother and embraced him. "I'm proud of you," Gryffin said. He let him go and patted him on the back. "I'll be with you every step of the way."

Marcus nodded, nervous about what he had to do but knowing fully well that Gryffin would always be there to help him through it. For the first time in a long time, Marcus didn't feel so alone. The brothers walked back to the stage door of The Lift. Gryffin told Marcus he was going to get Emery and take her home, and then they would drive to the police station together. Marcus agreed that he would wait by the car for them, seeing as he hadn't driven to The Lift in the first place.

Back in The Lift, Emery was getting steadily more worried about Gryffin. He hadn't come back yet. How long was he planning on following his brother? And how far? She kept glancing at the door, hoping he would walk through it. She felt someone tap her shoulder. Emery turned to see Gryffin in rough shape.

"Are you okay?" Emery exclaimed. He ran her fingers around the bruises and welts on his face. "What happened to you?"

"I'm okay." Gryffin held her shoulders to steady her. "We have to go right now. Okay? I'll explain everything to you in the car."

"Did you just come back in? I didn't see you come through the stage door."

"I was going to, but I would have attracted more attention from the crowd. I came in the front." Gryffin got Emery up from the bar and walked her to the restaurant entrance. He led her outside and to her car, where she saw someone waiting for them.

"Is that Marcus?" Emery inquired.

"Yeah, he's going to ride back with us, and then I'm going with him to the police."

"The police?" Emery stopped walking, forcing Gryffin to stop too. "What happened, Gryffin?"

"Marcus is going to turn himself in along with Dominic and all of the other people involved in his posse. He got ahold of some drugs that he was supposed to take to Dominic, and now he's going to take them to the police as evidence." Gryffin tried to explain as quickly as he could. "We can talk more in the car, but we have to go right now. There are some people who will be waking up soon, and when they do, they will not be happy."

Emery gave him a confused expression as Gryffin nudged her on toward her car.

When they reached it, Marcus gave Emery an uncomfortable half smile. He didn't look as beat-up as Gryffin, but he had definitely been in a fight. She unlocked the car. Gryffin quickly got into the passenger's seat and buckled up. Before Marcus could get in the back, Emery said, "You're a good man, Marcus Brooks. It takes a lot of courage and morality to turn yourself in."

Marcus's throat caught, and his stomach tightened. He slid in the backseat of the car and buckled in. Marcus knew what he was about to do was suicide, but Gryffin and Emery would be okay. That was all that mattered.

Chapter 21

*E*mery dropped Gryffin and Marcus off at Gryffin's car. Gryffin instructed Emery to drive around a bit more before going home. He wasn't sure if Kyle and Charles had reported what had happened back to Dominic yet or if they were even awake. Either way, he didn't want to take any chances. Emery did just that; she went around the block once, drove around town for a little while, and then went back home. Gryffin and Marcus went directly to the police station. Gryffin reported that he had been assaulted and held at gunpoint. Marcus confessed he was in league with Dominic and his drug trade. The chief investigator had a huge file on Dominic, and with the case full of drugs and a witness, he would finally be able to put Dominic away for good.

Gryffin stayed as long as he could with Marcus. But eventually Marcus had to go off on his own to be processed and locked up after all of the interviewing. Marcus asked an officer to let Gryffin know it was okay to go home. Gryffin waited in the lobby for a couple more hours just in case Marcus needed him. At four thirty in the morning, Gryffin decided to go home and get some sleep. He asked the officer at the front desk to be informed of any developments. The officer agreed to this and wished him a good morning. Gryffin went home feeling at ease. He sprawled out on the sofa and fell asleep in peace.

A court hearing was held, and Marcus was given a six-month prison sentence. It was so short because of his willingness to work with the police. Between the time he had turned himself in and the court date, the police had brought in Dominic and about 85 percent of his dealers, as well as anyone else who bought from him. Everyone else had left the state and gone into hiding. They weren't expected to be heard from for a very long time. Emery and Gryffin saw Marcus on the first visitor's day. It was strange to see him in an orange jumpsuit surrounded by bars. Everything in there was either a light gray or white. All the inmates who had visiting privileges were with their friends and families, catching up on time lost.

Emery and Gryffin sat across from Marcus at a table near the center of the room. Marcus looked good for being in prison. He was shaven, and his hair was short and kept, unlike the wild, tousled mop he had sported before. Marcus was so happy to see them; it felt like a lifetime had passed since the court hearing.

"Hey, little brother," he greeted Gryffin. "Miss." He winked at Emery.

"You look good, man," Gryffin took in the new and improved Marcus.

"I feel good," Marcus agreed. "Been working out a little here and there. Wanna be in shape when I leave this place and get back out there on the market."

Gryffin and Emery exchanged looks, unsure of what he meant by market.

"I mean dating market." Marcus realized what his wording may have sounded like.

"You want to get a girlfriend, huh?" Gryffin cocked an eyebrow. Marcus had dated around in high school but never anything serious. He was more about himself than anyone else. At least he used to be.

"Yeah, I want to meet someone and settle down after I serve my time here."

"What brought that notion?" Gryffin was curious.

Marcus answered truthfully, "I see how you two are together. Supportive and loving to one another. You love each other selflessly. I want to be able to love someone like that and, in return, have someone love me like that."

Emery felt warm inside. "I think you'll find someone who accepts and loves you just the way you are. And if they don't, they aren't worth your time. You're a great person, Marcus."

"Thanks, Emery." Now Marcus was getting all warm.

"So," Gryffin chimed in, "how is everything here?"

"It's okay. Dominic and most of his guys are at the state prison. But some of the less important people are here."

"Do they give you a hard time?" Emery asked.

"A little. But it's nothing I can't handle." Marcus didn't want them to worry. It really wasn't that bad. He had gotten hit a few times, been called names, and spat on, but he could take care of himself.

"You'll be home before you know it." Emery squeezed his hand. "Then you can find your dream girl."

"I may need a little help with that. Do you have any sisters?" Marcus joked.

"No, but there are plenty of girls out there for you to meet." Emery laughed.

"Well, keep an eye out for me in the meantime. I've still got a while." Marcus directed this to both of them.

"We'll see what we can do." Gryffin smirked.

The three of them talked the rest of the time Gryffin and Emery were permitted to stay. They talked about everything from movies to music to the interest Marcus had in finding a girlfriend. The time came for them to go. Emery and Marcus clasped hands, and Marcus told her to take care of his little brother. Marcus patted Gryffin's shoulder and said nothing. He just smiled. Emery and Gryffin waved as Marcus went back into the main part of the prison along with the rest of the inmates. Both of them had noticed something different about Marcus. Not his haircut or his new muscles. There was something different in his eyes. *Life.*

Chapter 22

While Marcus was in prison, Emery and Gryffin went every visitor's day to sit and talk to him. Marcus was doing well, and a newfound purpose oozed from within him. He couldn't wait to get out of there. The prison food was terrible, and he could hardly tolerate some of the other inmates, but he mainly wanted to leave to officially start his clean slate. Gryffin had never experienced a Marcus with drive and passion to do something. All of his prayers were being answered; his brother had finally manned up and taken responsibility. In a way, this was also Marcus dealing with the grief he had held onto for so long after the death of his parents. Gryffin and Marcus bonded in a way that they had never bonded as brothers before.

The next six months went by quickly for Emery and Gryffin. They were once again free to be together in public with no fear of being in harm's way. Most of the time they spent together was filled with picnics at the park, going to the field of music Gryffin loved so much, and just enjoying each other's company any way they could. The couple grew fonder of each other with each passing day. Gryffin was going to marry this girl one day; he was sure of it. Emery couldn't see herself with anyone else. Gryffin took care of Emery even though he knew she could take care of herself. Emery opened up to Gryffin about everything, even when it was something as minimal as being irritated over a driver who cut her off. Because of recent events, they blossomed in ways that average couples would not have in the short amount of time they had been together. They were connected in an unbreakable bond that would last a lifetime.

Escalates was booked every weekend, between bar shows and outdoor music festivals. Emery went to every show to support her friends. She stayed in the crowd to get the full band experience, and at every concert, she could see the fan base growing. They landed a show at a huge festival at the end of the summer. It was before their anniversary and a few days after Marcus's release. Marcus expressed during their visits how he was so excited to go and see the band again. He hadn't been to a show in years and was looking forward to seeing them all in action. Gryffin was pleased to hear Marcus was coming. He was even more pleased that his brother was changing for the better.

Emery and Gryffin were coming up on their ten-month anniversary. Gryffin couldn't believe that they had been together that long already. It felt like just yesterday that he was convincing her to stay and listen to his band that Friday night at The Lift.

Emery felt the opposite. She had been waiting for another landmark in their relationship. It felt like they had been together for ages, which was a good thing, but she needed moments of definition to know that they were actually going somewhere and not standing still. It was silly, and she knew it. The only other relationship she had been in, they didn't celebrate this sort of thing. Sure, ten months wasn't a milestone, but it was ten months she had spent with someone she loved dearly. And because Gryffin was Gryffin, every small step that they took needed to be commemorated. Emery wondered what he had planned for this anniversary.

On October 14, Marcus was released from jail. Gryffin waited for him outside in anticipation. When Marcus walked through the front gate in the clothes he had been wearing the night of the quarrel with Dominic's thugs, Gryffin greeted him with open arms.

He slapped Marcus's back hard. "How does it feel to take your first steps as a free man in six months?"

Marcus chortled, "Never been better, little brother." He slapped Gryffin's back too.

"Let's go home." Gryffin smiled broadly, happy to get his brother out of there.

"Yeah." Marcus felt like a million dollars. He was ready to try this new life thing.

The drive back to the apartment was a half hour. Marcus told Gryffin about how amazing it felt to be on the other side of the bars. He even asked Gryffin to turn on the radio. Gryffin flipped through the channels, unsatisfied with what was playing. Marcus told him to stop on a station when he recognized a tune. Marcus's face lit up, eyes darting to Gryffin.

"You know what this is?" Marcus asked in excitement, hoping Gryffin would remember.

Gryffin narrowed his eyes. "Of course I know this song." He acted appalled that Marcus would insinuate he had forgotten one of their favorite songs. "We listened to this on repeat for months when it first came out."

Marcus laughed and nodded in agreement. "Man, we would sing so loudly in the car that Mom would tell us to be quiet so she could concentrate on the road."

They both erupted in laughter, recalling how their mother would tilt the rearview mirror so she could see her sons and scold them for being too ornery. Gryffin mimicked his mother, which made Marcus laugh even harder.

"This is still a great song." Gryffin found himself humming along.

Marcus burst, quite loudly and off key, into song, pretending he was holding a microphone in his hand and serenading Gryffin. Gryffin joined right in, keeping his eyes on the road but pointing to Marcus during the appropriate parts of the song. The boys were having the best time reliving in the past. After the song ended, they popped in an old CD Gryffin still had and sang along with those songs too. The half-hour drive whipped right on past them. In no time, they were at the apartment with aching sides and sore cheeks.

Marcus stretched out on the couch that evening just like old times. Gryffin was happy his brother was home. Marcus, however, felt the obligation to tell Gryffin that he would be getting a job to help pay rent. Gryffin told him it wasn't a big deal, but Marcus insisted that he pull his own weight. Eventually, Marcus did want to get his own place, but for now he would act as if Gryffin were his landlord. He would have to work from the bottom and build himself back up again.

The next morning, Gryffin and Marcus had breakfast together. Marcus made scrambled eggs and toast, his specialty. During breakfast, Marcus remembered that Gryffin had an anniversary with Emery that was only a couple days away.

"Wow, that long already?" Marcus hadn't grasped that his little brother had been in a relationship for ten months already. "I guess that's what happens when you go away for six months. You lose your sense of time." Marcus chomped on a piece of burnt toast.

"I suppose." Gryffin twirled his fork in his scrambled eggs. "Can I run something by you, Marcus?"

"Of course." Marcus acted as if that was a stupid question.

"I have an idea for a gift for Emery," Gryffin began. "I wrote her another song, and I wanted to play it for her at the concert tomorrow afternoon. But this time I want her to be on stage with me. I really want to show everyone that I want her and only her. She's the only person I care about hearing my song."

"Sounds good. So what's the problem?" Marcus asked.

"Emery doesn't like being the center of attention. I don't want to embarrass her or make her feel uncomfortable."

"I see." Marcus wiped his mouth with a napkin. He placed it on his now empty plate. "Let me ask you this. Wasn't the whole purpose behind your meeting to get her to go outside of her comfort zone?"

"Yes."

"Then how is this different? From what you told me, she's doing things now that she would have never done when you first met. Emery is more outgoing now and willing to try new things. I really doubt she'll be upset with you if you call her on stage and dedicate a song to her. Besides, what girl doesn't want to be serenaded?"

Gryffin was impressed with Marcus's wisdom. He had a point. Emery wasn't the same girl he met ten months ago. She had broadened herself to take more chances and was generally happier. Still, doubt crept into Gryffin's mind.

"What if I call her to come on stage and she doesn't come up?" Gryffin feared.

"You leave that to me." Marcus jabbed his thumb at himself. "I'll get her up there. Just tell me what song and when you're playing it. I got it covered." Marcus was all about this surprise gift.

"Okay then, it's a plan." Gryffin liked Marcus's enthusiasm.

The two conspired the rest of the morning about the secret anniversary gift that was taking place the next day. Gryffin told him his plans for the actual anniversary day. He would take her on a picnic at the park they so often visited and give her another gift. When Gryffin told Marcus what the other gift was, Marcus gave him a sly smile.

"You romantic devil," he said to Gryffin.

"Shut up." Gryffin waved off his comment.

"Are you going to marry her?" Marcus asked abruptly.

The question caught Gryffin off guard. At the same time, he knew his answer right away. "Yes."

Marcus fist-pumped into the air. "I knew it!"

"Not right away but someday yes." Gryffin's face showed sheer glee.

"I'm glad you met her, Gryffin," Marcus said.

"Yeah, me too," Gryffin replied.

Marcus was happy he would gain such a great sister in the

future. Gryffin was ecstatic that he had met the girl he wanted
to spend the rest of his life with. And the best part about it was
that Emery chose him. She didn't have to, and she could change
her mind. But for now, she wanted to be with him and only him.
Gryffin prayed that that would never change.

Chapter 23

The day of the festival show arrived. Unlike his last show where he had played the song he had dedicated to Emery for the first time, Gryffin was not nervous. He was excited—thrilled to show the crowd this incredible girl he was in love with and express how much she meant to him. Gryffin wore his classic holey jeans and wore a sleeveless, black cutoff. He laced up his gray Converse and was ready for action. The band was meeting at the festival an hour early to get all of their equipment out and tuned. This was also a battle of the bands competition, so they wanted to hear who else was playing and what their odds were against them. Gryffin rushed around the house, grabbing his guitar cases and various cords he had to bring in case the ones that were already packed away went haywire. On all accounts, Gryffin was running late.

Gryffin buzzed Emery's apartment. She appeared downstairs soon after. She was dressed in jeans and an Escalates white T-shirt. A pair of reflective sunglasses rested atop her head. Today, Emery's hair had a wispier look to it, perfect for an outdoor summer concert. Gryffin grinned at her apparel choice.

"When did you get that?" He examined the shirt.

She flushed. "When you guys played the Middleton show. I told Paige not to tell you."

"Who knew you were so full of spirit?" Gryffin was moved by how supportive she was.

"I didn't," Emery replied with a snarky tone.

Gryffin pulled her in and kissed her gently. Emery gave a small smile, Gryffin's smile.

"Shouldn't we be going?" Emery came back to reality.

Gryffin wasn't there yet. "Hm?" Then the realization of his time constraint set in. "Oh, yeah. And we're late!"

Gryffin quickly opened Emery's car door for her and closed it behind her after she got in. Then he hurried himself into the driver's side of the car. They were on their way.

They reached the festival two hours later after listening to music and talking the whole ride there. The battle of the bands was being held at a campground where they saw many trailers and tents set up. It was quite the turnout for the show. Gryffin and Emery passed many people walking to the stage and crowding around it as they drove on the paved road to get to the reserved parking for the band members. They pulled in next to Derek's SUV. Derek and Alec were unloading an amp when Gryffin parked the car. Alec was wearing a dark red muscle shirt, appropriate for showing off his biceps as he always did. Derek wore a plaid black-and-white button-up and black skinny jeans with a bandana tied around his head. Once again, Alec was clearly the best dressed.

Emery said hi to the guys and then went and looked for

Paige. While she was gone, Gryffin went over the plan for the last song one more time. Derek and Alec were excited for Gryffin, wanting to make this the best performance for him yet. Gryffin helped the guys take out the rest of the equipment, setting the amps to the side of the van so they wouldn't be in any car's way. The drum set was next to be unloaded out of the van. Typically, Paige would take care of most of that part; she was particular about people touching her drum set. However, she was nowhere to be seen.

"Where's Paige?" Gryffin asked Derek and Alec.

Alec gave Derek a questionable look. "You wanna tell him?"

"Nah, he'll find out for himself," Derek replied.

"What does that mean?" Gryffin's mind wandered to a scenario where Paige had quit the band.

"She's by the main stage," Alec said cryptically.

Gryffin walked off in the direction of the stage. Alec and Derek laughed as if they were up to something.

The main stage was surrounded by people. This was the biggest crowd that Escalates had ever played for. Men, women, and children all gathered in one place with one purpose—to enjoy the music. Music brought people together in a way that intrigued Gryffin. He loved the unity they all shared, having the love and passion for the same thing.

To the side of the stage, the one closest to Gryffin, he saw Emery and Paige with their backs turned, watching the band currently playing their set. Paige wore her white high-top sneakers, shorts, and a red tank top. She was talking to someone next to her, and closely too, Gryffin noticed. The man was a tad taller than Gryffin and wore a green T-Shirt with khaki shorts. It was Marcus. Marcus had driven up with Alec in the band van so he could give Emery and Gryffin some time alone on the ride up. He and Paige seemed to be having a hilarious conversation because Paige kept giggling. Emery caught sight of Gryffin over her shoulder and went to him. She noted the odd look he had on his face seeing his brother and longtime friend flirting.

"I know, it's weird," Emery agreed. "But they seem to be getting along really well."

"How did that even happen?" Gryffin tried to wrap his mind around the phenomenon he was experiencing. He had never seen Marcus talk to a girl like that before. Then again, he had never seen Paige talk to a guy like that before.

"Paige told me that he came to help set up, and he started asking her about how it was being a girl drummer and said he thought her hair was really cool. I don't know, but Paige seems to like him." Emery replied.

"Interesting." Gryffin wasn't sure how to feel.

"I guess Marcus's plan to try to find a good girl to settle down with is actually working." Emery was as surprised as Gryffin, but she was happy for Marcus. Marcus deserved someone sweet and kind like Paige after all he had been through. If he was going to find someone who accepted him for all of the things he had done in the past, she was the ideal candidate.

Paige and Marcus clapped after the band finished a song. Seeing Emery and Gryffin standing behind them, they walked over cheerfully and joined their friends.

"Hey, I was coming to tell you that we're ready to unload your set," Gryffin informed Paige.

"Okay, thanks." She turned to Marcus. "Would you mind helping me set it up?"

"Not at all." Marcus was happy to help her out.

"By the way, we've been checking out the competition, and I think we're going to be just fine." Paige winked.

"I still want to play our best," Gryffin retorted. He didn't want Paige to feel like she didn't have to try. Today's show was important.

"I know, but I'm just saying. Most of the people here are *our* people." She motioned to the crowd.

Gryffin felt a sweep of comfort. "Okay, I feel pretty good then," he admitted.

"We'll see you guys soon." Paige took Marcus's hand and pulled him along behind her.

Marcus went willingly, giving Gryffin a thumbs-up as he passed him. Emery laughed, and Gryffin shook his head, chuckling at his brother's latest achievement.

Two bands went on before Escalates' slot in the showcase. The band members, along with Emery and Marcus, watched them intently. They also watched the reaction of the crowd when the bands played. The audience cheered after every song for both bands. But the first band's cheers were especially loud. Derek and Paige figured that this band would be their biggest competition for the contest. The second band was all right; it was more punk rock than anything. The crowd didn't seem as interested in them as the first band, which had a more folky sound. Gryffin, Emery, Derek, Alec, Paige, and Marcus still enjoyed listening to both of them, not being skeptical or smack-talking their competitors. It was about the music anyway, not the title of first prize. Although none of them would complain if they ranked first.

Finally, Escalates was called onto the stage. The crowd roared mightily for them, chanting their name as they suited up to play. Paige was right; the majority of the crowd did come for Escalates. Emery was especially excited for this show. This was the largest audience the band had ever had, and it was a competition. And Emery really wanted them to win. She stood with Marcus on the side of the stage where only the band members and crew were allowed.

When the band was all plugged in and warmed up, Gryffin walked up to the microphone and shouted excitedly, "We are Escalates! Everyone, have a great time today!" Gryffin introduced the band the same way every time.

The band was only playing two songs. The first one Emery knew, but the second one she had no idea about. When she had asked all of them, they responded with, "We haven't figured that one out yet." Or, "We have to do two songs?" Either way, Emery hoped they had a plan.

And have a plan they did.

The first song they played was meant to get the crowd up and jumping, which it did. Gryffin played his electric guitar hard and sang with his heart. Derek jumped along with the audience members, and Alec just rocked out on his guitar. Paige did stick tricks and sang along to the song. They were all having so much fun on stage, causing the audience to have a great time as well.

Marcus hadn't heard his brother play in years. He was blown away by their performance and even more by the fact that Gryffin, his little brother, had written the song. Emery clapped along and sang the lyrics, knowing them by heart after all of the times she had heard it during other shows. This song was definitely the crowd favorite at every venue. Emery was glad that they decided to play it here today.

When the first song ended, Gryffin thanked the crowd for their participation, saying that they were amazing and so great for coming out that hot day. Marcus was in midclap when his eyes became wide with worry. Emery saw Marcus pat his pocket, reach in, and pull out a pick.

"Oh no, I totally forgot to give this back to Gryffin before he went on!" he frantically said.

"What? Well, go give it to him!" Emery pushed him toward the stage.

"I can't!" Marcus cried.

"Why not?" Emery didn't see any reason why he couldn't.

"I have serious stage fright. If I go up there, I'll be sick!" Marcus pleaded. "You have to take it up there."

Emery glanced on stage. Gryffin was patting his pockets searching for his pick. She couldn't let him down. With a sharp breath of exasperation, she snatched the pick from Marcus's hand. "You so owe me for this."

"Thank you so much! You won't regret this!" Marcus yelled after Emery as she walked up the stage steps.

Out on the stage, in front of around hundreds of people, Emery felt a bit nervous. She wasn't going to perform or even talk, but she still had an uneasy feeling as she walked to the center of the stage to where Gryffin was standing. Gryffin wasn't searching for his pick anymore. He was watching Emery. As she walked by Derek, he gave her a smirk like something was about to happen. Emery no longer trusted the situation. The crowd was talking amongst themselves, some still hollering and whooping for Escalates, but they all watched her make her way to Gryffin.

Gryffin was beaming. Emery put out her hand for Gryffin to take the pick from her to play the final song. Instead, he took her whole hand in his and then addressed the crowd.

"Everyone, I want to share something very special with you," Gryffin began. Emery felt a knot in her stomach. "This is Miss Everett, the girl I am in love with."

The crowd whistled and clapped.

"We have been together for quite some time now," he continued. This was followed by more cheering. "I know she doesn't like attention or being in front of this many people. But," he directed this at Emery, "I want everyone to know how much you meant to me. That's why I wrote this song for you. And I want you to stay here with me, so I can sing it to you. Because you're the only person I want to make sure hears it."

Emery blushed, tears coming to her eyes. *Is this real?* Gryffin kissed the top of her hand that he was holding and then let it go, taking the pick. He turned from her to set down his electric guitar to pick up his powder-blue acoustic. He slung it over his shoulder and plugged it into the amp. Gryffin then began plucking the strings, a beautiful melody, which the full band would play during the second half of the song. Emery listened intently, still unable to fathom that this was really happening to her.

Gryffin began to sing.

I see the city lights.
I see a million smiles.
They are nothing compared to yours.
I feel the summer breeze,
I feel these hearts beat.
They're nothing without you here.

Paige did a roll on the ride cymbal into the chorus of the song.

Feel the leaves brush your skin.
Feel the rain; let it sink in.
Baby, you're the reason that I sing,
Find the words to ease my pain.
Without you, I'd go insane.
Baby, you're the dream inside my soul.

Gryffin looked straight at Emery.

This is the rest of our lives.

The band kicked in now, building more depth to the song.

Crazy how this life goes by.
Crazy how there is so little time.
I wanna spend every moment with you.
Love turns this world around.
Love keeps you safe and sound.
I'll spend all my days loving you.

He stood to the side of the microphone so he could sing into it while looking at Emery.

Feel the leaves brush your skin.
Feel the rain; let it sink in.
Baby, you're the reason that I sing,
Find the words to ease my pain.
Without you, I'd go insane.
Baby, you're the dream inside my soul.

The band went to the bridge, building up the song more.

Take your time to breathe me in.
I'll give you faith, no sink or swim.
Baby, make my heart pound under this sun
For the rest of our lives.

Gryffin stopped playing his guitar as the rest of the band continued. He let it hang on his back as he took the mic out from the
holder on the stand and went to Emery. He took her hand and
placed it on his chest so she knew, without a doubt, that this song
was for only her.

Feel the leaves brush your skin.
Feel the rain; let it sink in.
Baby, you're the reason that I sing,
Find the words to ease my pain.
Without you, I'd go insane.
Baby, you're the dream inside my soul.

This is the rest of our lives.

Gryffin held the mic between them so he could rest his head on
Emery's.

You are the rest of my life.

The band gave one final strum, and Paige crashed on the cymbals a few times before it officially ended.

Emery couldn't hear the crowd going ballistic for the song. She didn't see Alec, Derek, and Paige go out to the edge of the stage and throw band merchandise out to the audience. Emery only saw Gryffin. She only wanted to see Gryffin. The crowd, the band members, everyone was in black and white. Gryffin was in color. Everything was faded but him. Gryffin kissed the top of Emery's forehead and smiled down at her. Her cheeks were wet from the emotion he had brought out in her through the song. *Their* song.

"Happy early anniversary, Miss Everett." Gryffin spoke quietly.

"I love you too." She sniffled.

Gryffin stroked her hair and brought her to him, hugging her tightly. The crowd was still going wild. Over Emery's shoulder, Gryffin could see that even the other bands were cheering for them. Marcus gave him a nod in approval. Gryffin smiled, thanking him silently.

The stunt that Gryffin and his bandmates pulled ended up winning them first place in the contest. It seemed that the judges had a soft spot for young love. The band won a check for five hundred dollars and a large trophy that had Battle of the Bands—First Place inscribed on it. Escalates went out for an encore after they accepted their award. Emery was still awestruck by what Gryffin had done. The whole band had been in on it. Marcus even admitted to her that he didn't really have a problem with stage fright. This resulted in Emery giving him a playful punch to the arm. Escalates played another upbeat song Emery enjoyed. There wasn't one song that Emery didn't like from them.

They finished the song and hopped off stage. Packing up their equipment went quickly with everyone helping. That and the adrenaline from the show made them move faster. They all decided to walk around the campground for a bit and just relax. Marcus and Paige split from the group halfway through their walk and went to get ice cream at the camp store. Alec, Derek, Gryffin, and Emery found a vacant volleyball court and played the most fun yet intense game of volleyball Emery had ever been a part of.

Later that evening, Paige and Marcus met up with the rest of the band and Emery. A group of campers who just happened to be huge fans of the band invited them back to their campsite for a fire and some food. Derek was the first to accept the offer for everyone when he heard the word food. They spent the rest of the night at the campsite with people they rarely knew but actually liked to hang out with. Emery and Gryffin sat in front of the fire while everyone bustled about making s'mores and playing corn hole.

"Thank you," Emery whispered to Gryffin,

Gryffin put his arm around Emery and let her lean into him, resting her head on his shoulder. Gryffin had never felt so alive in his life.

Chapter 24

The morning of October 16 arrived. Gryffin had turned in right when they got home from the campground last night. He wanted to be well rested and prepared for today's festivities. Even though he wasn't doing anything spectacular for Emery, Gryffin wanted today to be memorable.

He got out of bed, showered, and got dressed. Today was special, so Gryffin dressed the park—black pants and nice shoes that would shine in the sun, along with a blue, button-up, collared shirt. He then made sure that Emery's gift was ready to go; that was the most important thing next to actually spending time with his girlfriend. Gryffin then went to the kitchen to prepare the picnic he would take with them to the park.

Gryffin's menu for lunch was as follows: salads with ranch dressing and croutons, followed by the main course of chicken Alfredo pasta, and then a trip to a small ice-cream joint five minutes from the park to end the meal. He prepared everything in the kitchen that morning, keeping the chicken Alfredo pasta heated in a travel container that was designed to do so. He put everything in the picnic basket along with plates, napkins, silverware, and two bottles—one full of sweet tea for Emery, and the other was cola for Gryffin. Gryffin went to the closet next to the front door and pulled out a large, plaid, red and blue blanket. He made sure it didn't smell musty from being in the closet for so long. Not such scent came to Gryffin's nostrils. Gryffin tucked the folded blanket under his arm and picked up the picnic basket, making his way to the front door.

"Hey, wait a minute." Marcus stopped him at the door.

Gryffin halted and looked questionably to Marcus. "What?"

"Just have a good time today. And congratulations," Marcus said.

"Thanks, brother." Gryffin smiled. "I'll see you later tonight."

"All right. Tell Emery I said hello." Marcus held the door open for Gryffin.

"I will. See you." Gryffin said good-bye and was out the door, Marcus closing it behind him.

Gryffin went to his car and put the key in the trunk lock to pop it open. When he had done so, Gryffin carefully placed the picnic basket up against the side of the trunk. He then rolled up the blanket and tucked a little under the basket, making a blockade to prevent the basket from swerving when Gryffin turned a corner. He closed the trunk and was about to go to the front seat of his car when he heard a voice from behind him.

"Where is he?" a man's voice boomed.

Gryffin slowly turned to see Charles standing behind him. He had a gun pointed at Gryffin.

"Take it easy, man." Gryffin put his hands out like he meant no foul play. "Who are you looking for?"

"Marcus! I want Marcus!" Charles's eyes were wild with fury. He shook the gun at Gryffin, demanding an answer.

"I don't know, Charles," Gryffin lied. "I haven't seen him since he got out of jail."

"Liar! I know he's staying here!" Charles screamed, holding the gun under Gryffin's chin. "Tell me where he is *right now*!"

Gryffin would not give his brother up. "I don't know!"

"I'm right here, Charles!" Marcus yelled from the balcony above them. "Let Gryffin go. It's me you want." He walked cautiously down the apartment complex stairs.

Charles spat in Gryffin's face before he removed the gun from under Gryffin's chin. Gryffin waited for Charles to turn his back to him before wiping the saliva off of his face. Charles walked like he was drunk. Gryffin wasn't sure if it was because he really was under the influence or if he was just that angry. He waved his gun between Marcus and Gryffin so that neither of them would try to be a hero. Marcus held his hands up, ready for whatever Charles was about to do to him.

"Do you know how much I lost because of you?" Charles gave a maniacal laugh. "Do you know what you cost me after you turned in Dominic?"

Marcus didn't answer; he didn't think it was a good idea to.

"I lost my money, my house, and worst of all, my stash!" Spit shot from his mouth as he yelled.

Marcus saw that Charles had not had a fix in a couple of days. That was why he was acting so out of sorts and irrational. Charles was scary enough, without the added element of being addicted to something he was unable to get a hold of anymore.

"All because you couldn't shoot him." Charles pointed the gun back to Gryffin, who froze.

Gryffin had inched his way around Charles as he was talking, and now he was only a few feet from Marcus; both brothers were facing Charles together now.

"You destroyed everything we worked for!" He was crying now. Then he suddenly stopped. Charles looked back down at the gun. "Dominic would kill you if he was here." The hysterics were kicking in now, a huge teeth-filled smile plastered on his face. "So I'll just do it for him."

Charles aimed the gun at Marcus, who stood like a rock. If this was the punishment he had to take for what he had done, he would accept it willingly. Gryffin wouldn't have that though.

Marcus closed his eyes, ready to be hit. Gryffin jumped in front of Charles, grabbing the top of the gun and shoving it down toward the ground. Marcus heard a gunshot. He opened his eyes and looked down at himself. Nothing. No bullet wound. He had heard the shot though. Then a cold, terrible thought came into Marcus's mind. He looked to where Gryffin was standing before he had shut his eyes. Gryffin wasn't there anymore.

Gryffin was on the ground in front of him, motionless.

Charles's gun was pointed to the ground now. He was staring at Gryffin on the ground, not understanding what had happened. With the realization that he had shot Gryffin instead of Marcus, Charles knew his only option was to run. He had shot the wrong brother. Marcus saw Charles bolt. He didn't chase after him. He ran to Gryffin's side, dropping on his knees next to his little brother.

Gryffin was lying on his side, turned to the ground. Marcus took his shoulder and pushed him to lay fully on his back. That's when Marcus saw it.

Gryffin's stomach was pooling out blood.

"No, no, no." Marcus's head began to spin. He patted Gryffin on the face to keep him awake. "Stay with me, brother. Okay? You need to stay awake."

Gryffin's eyes were half-open, and he was groaning in pain. Marcus unzipped his hoodie and wrinkled it up into a ball, pressing it down on Gryffin's wound. He took out his cell phone from his back pocket and dialed 911.

"Hello, I need an ambulance at the Sunnyside apartment complex! There's been a shooting! Please hurry!" Marcus hung up and dropped the phone on the concrete, placing both hands on the garment soaking up Gryffin's blood.

"Marcus …" Gryffin could barely speak.

"Shh, save your energy. You're going to be okay." Marcus gathered all the strength he had to keep himself together.

"I need you to give her this." Gryffin's hand slowly slid into his jeans pocket and came out with a folded piece of paper. "And make sure she gets my present." He huffed. "I worked hard on that." Tears were falling from Gryffin's eyes.

Marcus cried too but remained hopeful that his brother would be okay. He took the paper from Gryffin's hand. "You can give it to her yourself. I'll hold onto it for you, okay?"

Gryffin coughed up blood. His breaths were getting wispier and slower. "Watch her for me, Marcus." His eyes were blinking slower now. Gryffin mustered up one last long breath to be able to say what he needed to say to Marcus before he left. Gryffin put his hand out for Marcus to take. Marcus took it and held tightly. Then Gryffin said, "I'm proud to call you my brother."

"I love you, Gryff," Marcus got out through the tears.

Gryffin gave his last award-winning smile that he was known by many for. His body relaxed then, and his head turned and rested on the ground. Marcus loosened his grip on Gryffin's hand. It fell, lifeless, from his grasp.

"Gryffin?" Marcus called him.

No answer.

"Gryffin!" Marcus cried.

No movement.

"No, no, don't go!" Marcus took his brother in his arms and cradled him. He shook from crying unbearably hard. "We need you, brother!" Marcus's voice was hoarse. In the distance, he heard sirens coming their way. Sirens that were too late.

Chapter 25

*E*mery bounced around her apartment as she got ready for her picnic with Gryffin. She wore a red summer dress with gladiator-style white sandals. She wore her hair half-up and half-down to keep her bangs out of her face. Today was going to be an extraordinary day; she could feel it. Emery made sure she had her purse, checking the contents for the present she was going to give Gryffin. She felt around inside and pulled out a small, square white box with a black bow tied around it. Emery was proud of herself for coming up with the idea for this gift. She tucked it back in her purse and waited for Gryffin to come for her.

At 1:45, Gryffin had not yet come. Emery had texted and called him and Marcus multiple times to see what was taking him so long. She sat on the couch, impatiently waiting for any explanation as to why her boyfriend was an hour late picking her up. Emery got a strange feeling. One she couldn't quite explain. It was a sharp pain in her chest, like the muscles around her heart were tightening up, making it hard for her to breathe. She couldn't understand what it was, so she took some pain reliever for it, hoping it would go away by the time Gryffin got there. At 2:15, the buzzer sounded from downstairs. *Finally!* Emery hopped up from her couch and rushed out of her apartment in a flash.

Downstairs, Emery opened the front door to see Gryffin's car parked in its usual spot. Gryffin was usually leaning against it on the passenger side as he waited for her. This time, Gryffin was not there doing that. It was Marcus. Emery was surprised to see Gryffin's brother in his place. She walked over to him, looking around for Gryffin.

"Hey, Marcus. Where's Gryffin?"

It was then that Emery saw Marcus's face. His eyes were swollen, and his cheeks and nose were red. His eyes were glassy, and the area surrounding them was wet. The feeling Emery had earlier rushed back.

Emery was scared by Marcus's uneasy silence, "Marcus, where is Gryffin?"

Marcus looked to the ground, unable to face Emery. He shook his head. He then took a deep breath and brought his eyes back to Emery. "He's dead, Emery."

Everything stopped. The sounds around Emery were muffled, and her vision became blurry. Emery felt herself step backwards, water coming to her eyes. She tried to speak, but no words would come out. A wave of shock and anguish hit her.

"What ... no, he's going to come here ... he's picking me up for lunch." Emery couldn't make sense of what Marcus had said.

"He's not coming, Emery." Marcus took Emery's shoulders to hold her still. "He died trying to save me."

Emery could see in Marcus's eyes that he was deathly serious. That's when it hit her.

Gryffin was dead.

She would never be able to talk to him again.

He wouldn't sing anymore.

Gryffin was gone *forever*.

Emery cried out for Gryffin, and her entire body shook in grief. Marcus held her tightly as she wailed. Emery couldn't keep herself up; she began falling to the sidewalk. Marcus went down with her, steadily, sitting with her and crying with her.

The funeral showing was held two days later at the same funeral home where the Brooks' parents were shown when they passed away. Derek, Paige, and Alec were there along with people Emery did not recognize—people Gryffin must have met at shows or graduated high school with. It was strange to see all of the people dressed in black, and she supposed that was because it made the reality of the situation all the more real. Emery hadn't gone in to see the body yet. She couldn't bring herself to. Paige sat with her by the entrance. They didn't say much. Paige sat there for moral support, which Emery was thankful for. Marcus wasn't able to spend much time with her since he was in charge of the showing. He had to stay by Gryffin's body and talk to the visitors as they came up to pay their respects. Marcus went and checked on Emery every other hour. Emery would say she was fine, but Paige would tell him otherwise.

Derek and Alec told Paige they were leaving about ten minutes before the showing concluded. Emery insisted that she go with them. Paige have her a long hug and told her to call if she needed anything. Emery said she would and waved good-bye as they left. Marcus walked back to the front of the funeral home, where Emery had been sitting the entire time. A group of people exited as Marcus came up and sat with Emery.

"That was the last of them," he said.

"It was a good turnout. I mean … under the circumstances," Emery heard herself say. "A lot of people cared about him."

"Not as much as you though. Why don't you go in and say good-bye? You won't be able to if you don't go and do it now."

Marcus had a point. Emery didn't want to see Gryffin like this, but she did want to say good-bye one last time before he was buried tomorrow.

"I'll stay here, give you some privacy." Marcus touched her shoulder.

Emery nodded and stood. Marcus watched her leave and go into the main room. When she was out of sight, Marcus buried his head in his hands and wept.

The main room of the funeral home was furnished in beige and scarlet. The walls were bland, with various photos of the care-takers and layouts of the building, and the carpet was dark red with flourishes of yellow. Chairs sat in the middle and on either side of the room. Plants were in every corner and on every end table. To Emery, it was the gloomiest place on Earth.

Emery walked through the room, to the very front. She could

see Gryffin there, lifeless and dressed in a fine suit, lying in a coffin. Emery stopped. She took a quivering breath and straightened her long-sleeved black dress. Focusing on the task at hand, Emery moved forward. She made it to the coffin without crying, which was a shock to Emery. She had barely been able to go five minutes without breaking down. Emery saw him then, up close. Gryffin's hair was combed over, not messy as it usually was. His black suit and tie were perfectly ironed, and his hands were folded together on his stomach. Emery thought they did a good job making him look this way for his showing. Gryffin would have had something to say about it if he were here though. She knew exactly what it would be.

Out of her large purse, Emery pulled out Gryffin's favorite pair of Converse. She felt it was only right that he be buried with them. He would have hated to be wearing dress shoes forever. Emery set them on top of the closed lower portion of the coffin.

"I thought you might like to have those," Emery said. "You wouldn't want to be stuck in those dress shoes they have you in." She laughed to herself in remembrance.

"I have something else too," Emery continued. She took out the same white gift box she had put in her purse a few days ago. She unwrapped it. "Remember when you said you lost your pick after that show at that old bar a few towns away?"

For some reason, Emery waited for him to answer. But he didn't. She knew he wouldn't.

She cleared her throat. "You blamed Derek for losing another one of your picks. Well," Emery opened the lid and took out a small silver-chained necklace with a navy blue and light blue speckled pick hanging from it. "I took it. I wanted to engrave it with the band's name on the front and yours on the back so Derek would

make sure to give it back after a show." She showed him the en-
graved band name in cursive letters on the front and his name in
the same font on the other side. "I was going to give this to you
for ..." Emery trailed off.

She felt the tears building up. Her throat was catching. She
swallowed hard and then began to cry. "I miss you, Gryffin. I want
you to know something else ..." She retrieved the folded paper
Marcus gave her the day she found out Gryffin had passed. The
same paper Gryffin told Marcus to give to her. She unfolded it and
held it out in front of him as if he could see it.

It was the list:

1. Enjoy the beauty of the world around you.
2. Laugh no matter your troubles.
3. Watch the world go to sleep.
4. Make a chain reaction.
5. Watch the world awaken.
6. Make room for new memories.
7. Step out of your normal.
8. Experience a miracle.

There were checkmarks on numbers one through seven, with
little side notes scribbled next to certain tasks. For example, the

word *carnival* was next to number two, and the word *fireworks* was sketched next to number four. Emery addressed the last task, the task that was untouched by a checkmark through it. Only a four words resided next to it: *She is my miracle.*

When Emery first saw it, she was taken back by it. How had she been *his* miracle? He didn't need saving. Gryffin was perfect. Emery pointed to item number eight on the list in front of Gryffin.

"You were my miracle, Gryffin Brooks," Emery said between sobs. "And I couldn't have asked for a better one." Her hand dropped, with the list in it, back down to her side. Her head was hunched over as she cried. From behind her, Marcus placed a hand on her back.

He gently took the necklace from Emery. "Gryffin would have wanted you to have this." Marcus unclasped it. "May I?"

Emery pulled her hair up for Marcus to put the necklace around her neck and clasp it in the back. She held the pick in her hand tightly after Marcus had finished fastening it together.

"He was the noblest person I ever knew," Marcus said.

"He was a lot of things," Emery agreed. "All of them were wonderful."

Marcus and Emery stood in front of the coffin a while longer before saying good-bye to their loved one a last time. They left, arms around each other, remembering all of the time they got to spend with Gryffin Brooks.

Chapter 26

The funeral for Gryffin Brooks was the most excruciatingly painful thing Emery Everett had ever experienced. The sky was overcast and dreary with no wind. Just dead air. It was as if God Himself was in mourning. Emery could barely make it through the service. She kept herself from sobbing uncontrollably at the burial site. Marcus stood strong for her, letting her lean on his shoulder when she couldn't keep herself up. People Emery didn't know gave her their sincerest condolences. Marcus said that this was because they knew how much she meant to Gryffin. Oddly enough, it was a refreshing sense of wholeness Emery felt, knowing that all of these people in mourning were there for her through this difficult time. She wouldn't have to bear this alone.

After the funeral, the gatherers had lunch that was provided at a hall that Marcus had rented for the occasion. The band played a few songs in Gryffin's honor, knowing that he would have wanted it to be a celebration of his life. Emery was glad that Escalates performed for Gryffin. She felt somewhere, up there, Gryffin was playing right along with them.

Later that afternoon, Emery and Marcus went back to the Brooks' apartment. Neither of them wanted to be alone. Marcus made coffee and set a mug out in front of Emery on the table. They stared blankly in their cups, wishing they were meeting under better circumstances.

"It's so weird, him not being here," Marcus said. His eyes were resting on something behind Emery.

Emery followed his gaze to Gryffin's opened bedroom door. "Yeah, I can imagine it would be."

Marcus slid his chair from under the table and stood. He stuffed his hands in his pockets as he walked over to Gryffin's room and went inside. Emery wasn't sure whether to follow him or let him be. She decided Marcus might need some time alone in his brother's old room.

"Gryffin told me to make sure you got this," Marcus said as he emerged from Gryffin's room. He carried a silver box with a red bow wrapped tightly around it. He set it down on the table in front of Emery. "This was the present he would have given you. Before he died, he said you needed to have it because he worked hard on it."

Emery let out a small chuckle; that did sound like what Gryffin might say. She unwrapped the box and lifted the lid. She reached inside and withdrew the contents of the box. Emery knew instantly what it was. She pulled out a large stack of photos—photos that Gryffin had taken on the disposable camera when they took their trip to his hideaway in the woods. Nostalgia overcame Emery.

"This was when Gryffin showed me the fort you guys made

deep in the woods," she explained to Marcus as she looked through the photos. Marcus sat beside her and looked at them with her. "He told me he was going to use up all the film." She smiled. Emery held up one of the photos a little higher than the rest, catching the light. She noticed something was written on the back of it. Turning it around, Emery saw the words *I wondered* written in black marker. She looked at the back of the next photo. This one said *right then*. Emery recognized this line.

"Help me put this together," she said to Marcus. Marcus already knew what the gift was, so he helped her turn over all of the photos and put them in order.

It took them about five minutes since there were so many photos to go through. They set them out on the table in the order Emery knew they went in. When they were done, Marcus and Emery reviewed their work. Sure enough, it was exactly what Emery thought it was.

Gryffin had written the lyrics of the first song he had ever written to her on the back of the photos.

Emery was amazed at how thoughtful this was. She was not surprised though; Gryffin had always been the sentimentalist. She turned back over every photo to take it all in. The very last photo on the table had a heart on the back of it. Emery turned it over to the photograph side to see Gryffin's favorite photo of Emery kissing him on the cheek in his car.

Emery sat back down in her chair. This was the greatest gift she had ever received. So thoughtful and meaningful. She sat back in her chair, expecting to cry again. Tears didn't come; instead, a smile did. "I'm glad I got to love him as long as I did," she said to herself.

Marcus took his seat next to Emery, hands folded on the table. He hesitated before asking her, "Do you mind if I see that paper he told me to give you?"

Emery didn't mind. She felt for it in her purse, retrieved it, and gave it to Marcus. Marcus opened it carefully, as it was very worn. When he had unfolded it completely, he took a long look at it. Emery watched his eyebrows scrunch together and his mouth quiver.

"What is it?" Emery put a hand on his arm.

Marcus set the paper out so they could both see it. "Gryffin made this list for me after the accident. He thought it would bring me out of my depression after they died. We did a few of them, but nothing worked."

It all made sense to Emery. The list hadn't originally been meant for Emery; it was meant for Marcus. Gryffin must have felt a sense of redemption when he was able to use it with Emery because he couldn't help his brother.

"It did work though," Emery said.

"What do you mean?"

"You changed, Marcus." She took his hands in hers. "You got better. You faced your guilt."

"The list didn't do that," Marcus corrected.

"No, but Gryffin did," Emery clarified. "And Gryffin made the list."

Tears rolled down Marcus's cheeks. She was right; Gryffin had helped him become a better man.

"You know what I think that sounds like?" Emery asked.

"What?" Marcus wondered.

"We both experienced a miracle." Emery realized that Gryffin's list really had worked. Not only for Marcus but for her. She got up and went to the other side of the counter where she knew Gryffin's junk drawer was. Emery fished for a pen, and when she found one, she went back to the table and put it in Marcus's hand.

"You should be the one to cross it off," she said quietly.

Marcus uncapped the pen and drew a red checkmark through number eight on Gryffin's list—the list that had changed both of their lives for the better.

Chapter 27

Eight Months Later

*E*mery was running terribly late. She had overslept once again, not hearing her alarm clock go off. Today she had to get up extra early before she went to work so she would have time to make a stop. Every Tuesday, she got up two hours earlier to meet a friend for coffee. Emery didn't have time to shower before she left, so she washed her face, brushed her teeth, did her hair hastily along with her makeup, and bolted out the door.

At the corner café in town, furnished in hardwood floors, white brick walls, and old furniture, Marcus Brooks waited for Emery at their usual spot. This had become their tradition a few weeks after Gryffin died. They remained close friends and wanted to keep in touch. Neither of them had any blood relatives anymore, so they adopted each other as honorary family.

Marcus ordered their usual when he got to the small café, a soy latte for Emery and a black coffee for himself. The air smelled of freshly brewed coffee and fresh baked pastries. Marcus was half-tempted to indulge in a blueberry muffin while he waited. Before he could reach a decision, he heard the doorbell chime, and Emery walked in.

"Hey, Emery." Marcus stood in courtesy as Emery came to her chair. When she sat, so did he.

"Hi, Marcus," Emery greeted, slinging her purse over the corner of her chair. She noticed the steaming cup of coffee before her. "Thank you. I owe you."

"No problem. So how's school?"

"It's going well." Emery thanked him for asking. Emery had enrolled in night classes at the community college. She was studying to become an elementary teacher. Gryffin had been right; she had a soft spot for children. Emery worked selling houses for the agency from the morning to the afternoon and then went straight to the college when she got off to do her schoolwork.

Marcus was proud of her. "I'm glad you talked yourself into it. You'll be a great teacher."

"Thank you. And how's the job?"

"It's all right. With my past, the best I can really do right now is a factory, so it works. I make decent money, and the hours aren't horrible," Marcus replied.

He had been working at an automotive factory for about a month now. He had a bit of a rough time getting back into a routine. But with Emery's help, he had landed a job and was volunteering at the high school as a counselor for kids with substance-abuse problems. Marcus hoped to make that a full-time job, but he needed money for schooling first. All in all, Marcus was doing well for himself.

"And you and Paige are official now. Congratulations!" Emery exclaimed. She was so happy they had gotten together. Paige was another reason Marcus decided it was time to keep moving with his life.

"Yeah, thanks." Marcus blushed a little. "I'm glad she found me, even in the midst of all the chaos."

"That's how you know it's worth it," Emery said, "when they stand by your side when you can't stand at all."

"She's an amazing girl. I hope it all works out, Emery. I really like her," Marcus replied.

"I think you'll be fine. I've seen how happy you are together," Emery assured him.

Emery and Marcus talked for a little while after that, finishing their coffees. When they were done, they hugged good-bye and went their separate ways, knowing they would see each other again the next Tuesday.

Escalates played shows now and again, but it didn't feel the same to them without their lead singer. Emery went to all of their shows. Derek was now the lead singer, and he made sure to sing at least one of Gryffin's songs about Emery and explain to the crowd each time the meaning behind it. Gryffin was remembered fervently by the fans as well. They brought signs that said he was never forgotten, and they talked to Emery about their favorite memories of him performing. Emery's family had extended to include Escalates and their entourage.

Emery hosted get-togethers every other month at her apartment with Marcus, Paige, Alec, and Derek. The importance of them keeping in contact was equal to everyone. They had all been through so much together in the last year, creating a bond that no one besides them would understand. When the band and Marcus came over, they would play cards, watch a movie, and sometimes the guys would bring their guitars and just jam. No one really cared what they did as long as they did it together. The friends Emery had always dreamt of having, she now had.

The loss of Gryffin still weighed heavily on Emery's heart. She looked through the photos he had given her often. The photograph of Emery kissing Gryffin's cheek was framed and sitting on her nightstand. Sometimes she found herself unknowingly holding the guitar pick on the necklace she never took off. A piece of Gryffin would always be with her.

Every now and again, when she needed a reminder to not become downhearted, Emery Everett would drive out to the field Gryffin had taken her to. She liked to think of it as *the enchanted field* because of the melody she could hear when she concentrated.

Emery got out of her car and walked to the middle of the field where Gryffin had first introduced her to the music. She stood and waited for a tune to sweep through the wheat and into her soul.

She heard the music.

The same tune she had heard when Gryffin helped orchestrate

it months ago. Emery waved her hands around and let the melody take control of her movements. Her hands went to and fro, gliding through the air. Emery looked up at the sky, smiling, feeling Gryffin smiling back.

Everyone has difficulties. Not one person goes through life un-scathed. It's what people decide to do about it. They can become consumed with hate and grief over how unfair life has been to them, shutting people out and neglecting themselves because of the hardships they have endured. Or they can do just the opposite, learning from their experiences and using them to help those who need it. They can take life as an adventure and one that is short and meant to be lived out, make something out of nothing and turn negatives into positives. God doesn't give us more than we can handle. It comes down to one defining question: will you hear the music?

About the Author

MIKAELA MUSSER wrote her first full-length story at age thirteen. In addition to writing, she also works as a photographer. She currently lives in Fremont, Ohio.

Printed in the United States
By Bookmasters